Shadows Over Cheyenne

A Novel

By Del Wilber

Copyright Page

Shadows Over Cheyenne

ISBN-Hardcover: 978-1-970330-00-7
ISBN-Paperback: 978-1-970330-06-9

First Edition: September 2025

Cover design by Book Cover Zone

Published by A. L. Wilber Jr
Website: delwilber.page

Printed in the United States of America

10 9 8 7 6 5 4 3 2

Dedication

For the storytellers who rode before me—

Larry McMurtry, who taught us that the West was beautiful and brutal in equal measure.

Cormac McCarthy, who showed us the darkness beneath the dust.

Charles Portis, who proved that honor and humor could share the saddle.

Elmore Leonard, who made every word count and every character matter.

Louis L'Amour, who kept the campfires burning for generations of readers.

And for all the Western writers, past and present, who understood that the frontier was never just a place—it was a proving ground for the human spirit.

This one's for you.

Ride on.

Table of Contents

Chapter 1: Winter's End in Cheyenne ... 1

Chapter 2: The Job Offer ... 12

Chapter 3: First Assignment ... 22

Chapter 4: Trail of the Rustlers ... 32

Chapter 5: The Other Side ... 42

Chapter 6: Deeper into the Territory ... 52

Chapter 7: Questions and Passion ... 62

Chapter 8: The Pattern Emerges ... 72

Chapter 9: The Puppet Master Revealed ... 80

Chapter 10: The Railroad Connection ... 89

Chapter 11: Carmen's Secret ... 98

Chapter 12: The Lakota Angle ... 109

Chapter 13: Caught Between Worlds ... 120

Chapter 14: Going Underground ... 130

Chapter 15: The Marshal's Dilemma ... 138

Chapter 16: Violence Escalates ... 149

Chapter 17: The Evidence ... 158

Chapter 18: The Trap Closes ... 167

Chapter 19: The Rescue ... 176

Chapter 20: Unlikely Allies ... 188

Chapter 21: The Shipping Season Showdown ... 198

Chapter 22: Justice Partially Served ... 209

Chapter 23: The Bitter Victory ... 220

Chapter 24: New Hope ... 233

Glossary: Western Terms ...245

Chapter 1: Winter's End in Cheyenne

The morning sun cut through the last of the winter clouds like a knife through canvas, and Cord McBride could feel the change in his bones. He stood in the doorway of Pete's Livery Stable, coffee steaming from the tin cup in his weathered hands, watching Cheyenne shake off winter like a dog coming out of a creek.

The street mud had that particular consistency that came with the spring thaw—thick enough to grab at a man's boots, but loose enough to splatter up to his knees if he wasn't careful where he stepped. Already, the early risers were picking their way through it, heading to the railroad yards where the real money got made in this town.

"Gonna be a busy season," Old Pete said from behind him, his voice carrying that rasp that came from too many years breathing stable dust. "Can feel it in the air, same as you can smell the snow leaving the mountains."

Cord nodded but didn't turn around. Pete's gimpy leg had been acting up all winter, but the old timer never complained. Just did what needed doing and kept his observations to himself most of the time. When Pete did speak, it was usually worth hearing.

"Town's been quiet too long," Cord said, taking another sip of the bitter coffee. "Feels like a pot about to boil over."

"That it does." Pete hobbled up beside him, favoring his left leg like always. "You staying on past the thaw?"

1

It was a fair question. Cord had been wintering in Cheyenne for three months now, doing odd jobs and keeping his head down. The arrangement with Pete had worked out well enough—Cord cleaned the stables and tended the horses in exchange for a dry place to sleep and whatever work Pete could throw his way. But they both knew it was temporary.

"Haven't decided yet," Cord said, which wasn't entirely true. His pockets held maybe fifteen dollars and some change, enough to get him down the trail but not far enough to matter. He'd been hoping something would turn up in Cheyenne, but so far the only steady work involved either the railroad or the cattlemen, and a man could get himself caught in the middle of that particular fight without meaning to.

The sound of hooves and wheels echoed off the false-fronted buildings as a freight wagon rumbled past, heading toward the Union Pacific yards. The driver gave them a nod as he passed, and Cord recognized him as one of the regulars who hauled supplies out to the smaller ranches northeast of town.

"Jake Morrison," Pete said, following Cord's gaze. "Good man, but he's been looking worried lately. Lot of the smaller ranchers have."

"Cattle rustling?"

"Some. But it's more than that." Pete shifted his weight, and Cord could see the old man was working up to something. "Word is, some of them herds that go missing turn up at the railroad pens a few days later. Different brands, different paperwork, but the same cattle."

Cord set down his coffee cup on the wooden rail that ran along the stable's front porch. He'd heard rumors all winter —conversations that stopped when he walked into a saloon, meaningful looks between men who thought they weren't being watched. But Pete was the first person to say it straight out.

"That's a serious accusation."

"It is. And the kind that can get a man shot if he's not careful who he says it to." Pete glanced up and down the street, then lowered his voice. "But between you and me, there's something rotten in this town, and it's got to do with who's buying cattle and who's asking questions about where they come from."

Before Cord could respond, the morning quiet was broken by the sharp blast of a train whistle from the yards. The 8:15 eastbound, right on schedule. In a few hours, that train would be loaded with cattle cars and heading toward the stockyards in Kansas City and Chicago, carrying beef to feed the growing cities back east.

"I better get these stalls mucked out," Cord said. It wasn't that he didn't want to hear more—it was that he'd learned to be careful about getting involved in other people's troubles. A man who'd survived Little Bighorn by being unconscious when the fighting started had learned something about the dangers of being in the wrong place at the wrong time.

But as he picked up the pitchfork and headed back into the stable, he couldn't shake the feeling that staying uninvolved might not be an option much longer.

The morning passed quickly enough. Cord worked his way through the stalls, cleaning and laying fresh straw, while Pete tended to the customers who came and went. A few drummers heading out to the smaller towns, a rancher's wife picking up her buggy horse, and a steady stream of railroad men checking on horses they kept stabled in town.

It was past noon when Cord decided to take a walk down to the stockyards to see what all the activity was about. The sound of cattle had been drifting up from the pens all morning, along with the shouts of men working the herds and the whistle of locomotives switching cars around the loading chutes.

The Cheyenne stockyards sprawled along the railroad tracks like a small city made of wooden corrals and chutes. Cattle filled the pens—longhorns from Texas, shorthorns from the local ranches, and mixed herds that could have come from anywhere between Mexico and Montana. The air was thick with dust and the smell of animals, and the constant lowing of cattle mixed with the shouts of cowboys and railroad workers.

Cord found himself a spot along the fence where he could watch the activity without getting in anyone's way. It was like watching a complicated dance—herds being sorted and moved, cattle cars being positioned and loaded, and paperwork changing hands between men in dusty work clothes and others in clean suits who never got closer to the animals than they had to.

He was watching a group of cowboys push a small herd of shorthorns toward a loading chute when he noticed something that didn't sit right. The cattle were moving wrong—not the tired, resigned shuffle of animals that had been in the pens for days, but the nervous energy of cattle that had been driven hard and recently.

And the brands didn't match.

Cord had a good eye for cattle brands, learned during his years drifting from ranch to ranch after the war. The herd moving toward the chute carried at least three different brands that he could see, but the paperwork being handed to the railroad loading boss showed only one.

He eased closer to the fence, trying to get a better look without drawing attention to himself. The cowboys pushing the herd were strangers—not the usual faces he'd seen around the ranches near Cheyenne. They worked efficiently, but there was something hurried about it, like men who wanted to finish a job and move on.

"Afternoon, stranger."

Cord turned to find a well-dressed man standing beside him, clean-shaven and wearing a suit that had seen better days but was still a cut above what most folks in Cheyenne could afford. The man's eyes were pale blue and calculating, and his smile didn't quite reach them.

"Afternoon," Cord replied, keeping his tone neutral.

"Haven't seen you around the yards before. You in the cattle business?"

"Just watching," Cord said. "New in town, trying to get the lay of the land."

The man nodded as if that made perfect sense, but his eyes flicked toward the loading chute where the mixed herd was being pushed into a cattle car. "Lot to see here. Cheyenne's become quite the hub for moving cattle east. Good business for everyone involved."

"I imagine so."

"Course, it takes the right kind of organization to make it all work smoothly. Can't have just anyone bringing cattle to market without proper documentation. Bad for business all around."

There was something in the man's tone that made it clear he wasn't just making conversation. Cord kept his expression neutral and nodded as if he understood perfectly, which in a way he did. He was being warned off.

"Makes sense," he said. "A man wouldn't want to interfere with legitimate business."

"Exactly." The well-dressed man touched the brim of his hat. "Enjoy your stay in Cheyenne, stranger. And remember—sometimes the best thing a man can do is mind his own business."

The man walked away, but Cord noticed he didn't go far. Just far enough to keep an eye on things while talking to another man who looked like he might be armed under his coat.

Cord stayed by the fence for another few minutes, watching the loading operation finish up. The mixed herd disappeared into the cattle car, the cowboys collected their money from the loading boss, and within an hour the whole operation had moved on to other pens and other herds.

But the feeling that he'd witnessed something he wasn't supposed to see lingered long after the train pulled out of the yards, heading east with its cargo of cattle that might or might not belong to the people who'd sold them.

As he walked back toward Pete's stable, Cord found himself thinking about the conversation he'd had with the old liveryman that morning. If what Pete suspected was true—if stolen cattle were being sold through the railroad —then what he'd just witnessed was part of something bigger than simple rustling.

And if that was the case, then staying uninvolved was going to be a lot harder than he'd hoped.

The sun was starting to sink toward the western mountains when he got back to the stable. Pete was sitting on the front porch, whittling a piece of pine and watching the street traffic thin out as the working day wound down.

"Learn anything interesting down at the yards?" Pete asked without looking up from his carving.

Cord settled onto the porch rail and thought about how much to say. Pete had been straight with him, and the old man deserved the same in return.

"Saw some cattle change hands that probably shouldn't have," he said finally.

Pete's knife stopped moving. "You sure about that?"

"Sure enough."

"Then you'd better be careful, son. This town's got a way of dealing with folks who see too much."

As if to emphasize the point, two riders came down the street at an easy lope, both wearing the kind of tied-down guns that suggested they knew how to use them. They slowed as they passed the stable, and Cord could feel their eyes on him even in the gathering dusk.

"Friends of yours?" he asked Pete.

"Not hardly. But I've seen them around town the past few weeks. They work for someone, but I couldn't say who."

The riders moved on, but the message was clear enough. Cheyenne might be a booming railroad town full of opportunities, but it was also a place where a man could find more trouble than he was looking for if he wasn't careful.

Cord watched the riders disappear around the corner toward the saloon district, then looked back at Pete, who had resumed his whittling as if nothing had happened.

"Pete," he said, "you know of any honest work in this town for a man who's not afraid of trouble but would rather avoid it if possible?"

The old man smiled for the first time all day. "Might be. Fellow came by earlier, asking if I knew anyone who might be interested in some investigative work. Government position, he said. Good pay, and the kind of job where a man with your particular experience might be useful."

"What kind of experience is that?"

"The kind that comes from staying alive when other folks don't."

Cord thought about that for a moment, remembering the weight of the Colt .45 under his coat and the skills that had kept him breathing through more fights than he cared to count. If there was government work available— legitimate work—it might be exactly what he needed.

"This fellow leave a name?"

"Said his name was Hayes. Captain Hayes. Told me he'd be at the Railroad House tomorrow morning around nine, if I knew anyone who might be interested." Pete paused in his whittling. "Claimed to represent territorial interests. Had the look of a man who's used to giving orders."

The Railroad House was the finest hotel in Cheyenne, the kind of place where territorial officials and railroad executives stayed when they came to town. If this Hayes was staying there and claiming government authority, he had money and connections, which could mean the work was legitimate.

Or it could mean something else entirely.

"Think I'll pay him a visit," Cord said.

"Figured you might." Pete folded his knife and slipped it into his pocket. "Captain seemed like the type who doesn't waste time on small talk. Said something about needing a man who could handle trouble along the railroad line. Mentioned decent pay and proper authority."

Cord's interest sharpened. Government work with a badge and territory to cover sounded like exactly the kind of legitimate opportunity he'd been hoping for. And if it involved investigating the cattle rustling he'd witnessed that afternoon, it might be a chance to do some good while earning an honest living. "Just remember what I told you about this town. Sometimes the line between the good guys and the bad guys isn't as clear as a man might hope."

As the last light faded from the sky and the oil lamps began to flicker on in the windows along the street, Cord found himself thinking about the cattle he'd seen that afternoon and the warning he'd received from the well-dressed stranger. Tomorrow he'd talk to this Captain Hayes and see what kind of work was being offered—and whether it might involve putting a stop to the rustling operation he'd witnessed.

But tonight, he had the feeling that his days of simply observing Cheyenne were coming to an end. Whether the job offer was legitimate government work or something else entirely, he was about to become part of whatever was happening in this town.

And after nine years of drifting and trying to stay out of other people's troubles, Cord McBride wasn't sure if that was the best thing that could happen to him, or the worst.

Chapter 2: The Job Offer

The Railroad House lobby smelled of leather, tobacco, and the kind of money that didn't worry about where the next meal was coming from. Cord pushed through the heavy oak doors at five minutes past nine, his boots echoing on the polished marble floor. Crystal chandeliers hung from the pressed tin ceiling, and thick Persian rugs covered the walking areas between clusters of upholstered chairs where well-dressed men conducted business in low voices.

It was the kind of place that made a man conscious of every scuff on his boots and every thread pulled loose on his coat. Cord had cleaned up as best he could at Pete's, but he still looked like what he was—a drifter with fifteen dollars in his pocket and nowhere particular to be.

"Help you, sir?" The desk clerk's tone was polite but carried the subtle message that if Cord was looking for work, he'd come to the wrong place.

"I'm here to see Captain Hayes. He's expecting me."

The clerk's eyebrows rose slightly, but he consulted his register with professional efficiency. "Ah yes. Captain Hayes mentioned he might have a visitor this morning. He's in the private dining room. Through those doors, first room on your right."

Cord nodded his thanks and made his way across the lobby, aware of the curious glances from the hotel's other guests. A few looked like territorial officials, others had the soft hands and clean clothes of railroad executives. All of them looked like they belonged here in a way that Cord never would.

The private dining room was smaller than the lobby but just as elegant, with dark wood paneling and oil paintings of mountain landscapes. A single table sat in the center, set with fine china and silver that caught the morning light from tall windows overlooking Cheyenne's main street.

Captain Benjamin Hayes stood with his back to the door, looking out at the street below. He was a tall man, well-built, with the kind of bearing that came from years of command. His dark hair was going gray at the temples, and when he turned to greet Cord, his eyes were the pale blue of winter ice.

"Mr. McBride, I presume?" Hayes extended his hand, and his grip was firm and confident. "Thank you for coming. Please, have a seat."

Hayes was dressed in a well-tailored suit of dark wool, with a gold watch chain draped across his vest. Everything about him suggested authority and success, from his polished boots to the way he moved with the easy confidence of a man accustomed to being obeyed.

"Coffee?" Hayes asked, settling into his own chair. Without waiting for an answer, he poured from a silver service into two cups. "I hope you don't mind meeting over breakfast. I find business discussions go better when men aren't distracted by empty stomachs."

"That's fine by me," Cord said, accepting the coffee. It was better than anything he'd tasted in months—rich and dark, without the bitter edge that came from boiling grounds too long over a camp fire.

Hayes studied him over the rim of his cup, and Cord had the uncomfortable feeling he was being measured in ways that went beyond his obvious lack of ready cash.

"Pete speaks well of you, ' Hayes said finally. "Says you're reliable, observant, and not inclined to ask questions that don't concern you. Those are valuable qualities in my line of work."

"What line of work would that be, Captain?"

"Law enforcement. Territorial law enforcement, to be specific." Hayes reached into his coat and produced a leather wallet, which he placed on the table between them. "I represent certain territorial interests that are concerned about the increasing lawlessness along the railroad corridors. Cattle rustling, in particular, has become a serious problem."

Cord thought about what he'd witnessed at the stockyards the day before. "I can see where that might be a concern."

"Indeed. The territorial government has decided to take action, but we need men who can work independently, cover large areas, and handle themselves in difficult situations." Hayes opened the wallet to reveal a silver badge, star-shaped and polished to a bright shine. "We're prepared to offer you a position as a special territorial detective, with particular focus on livestock theft along the railroad line."

The badge caught the morning light streaming through the windows, and Cord found himself staring at it. After years of drifting and taking whatever work he could find, the idea of legitimate authority—of being on the right side of the law for once—was more appealing than he cared to admit.

"What would the job involve, exactly?"

"You'd have jurisdiction along the Union Pacific line from Cheyenne north to the Nebraska border, and east into the areas where rustling has been most problematic. Your job would be to investigate reports of missing cattle, identify the thieves, and either arrest them yourself or coordinate with local law enforcement." Hayes leaned forward slightly. "The pay is sixty dollars a month, plus expenses. You'd be provided with proper credentials and would have the full backing of territorial authority."

Sixty dollars a month was more money than Cord had seen in one place since before the war. Combined with the promise of legitimate work and the chance to do some good, it sounded almost too good to be true.

"There must be plenty of men who'd want a job like this," he said carefully.

"There are. But most of them lack the particular qualifications we're looking for." Hayes's smile was thin but seemed genuine. "We need someone who can handle a gun but has the judgment to know when not to use it. Someone who can work alone for weeks at a time without losing sight of the mission. And frankly, someone who

15

understands what it means to survive when the odds are against you."

The last comment hit closer to home than Cord was comfortable with, but he kept his expression neutral. "Pete tell you much about my background?"

"Enough. You served in the Seventh Cavalry under Custer. You were at Little Bighorn." Hayes paused, watching Cord's reaction. "That tells me you've seen combat and survived it. In this job, that experience could be valuable."

Cord's jaw tightened slightly. The battle at Little Bighorn wasn't something he talked about, and he didn't appreciate having it brought up by a stranger, even one offering him work. But if Hayes knew about his military service, it suggested the man had done his research.

"I survived," Cord said simply.

"More than that. According to the records I've seen, you were commended for courage under fire on multiple occasions before Little Bighorn." Hayes reached for the coffeepot and refilled both their cups. "That's exactly the kind of man we need for this work."

Before Cord could respond, Hayes continued. "Your first assignment would be to investigate reports of missing cattle from ranches near Fort Collins. We've received word that several small ranchers in that area have lost significant numbers of livestock, and local law enforcement hasn't been able to make much progress."

Fort Collins was a good day's ride north of Cheyenne, in country Cord knew reasonably well. It was also close enough to the Nebraska border that rustlers could move stolen cattle across territorial lines before anyone noticed they were missing.

"You'd have a contact there," Hayes said. "Someone who can provide you with local information and help you get oriented. Telegraph operator named Delgado. Carmen Delgado. She's been keeping track of the situation for us."

A woman telegraph operator was unusual but not unheard of, especially in smaller towns where qualified men might be hard to find. The fact that she was working as an informant suggested she was both trustworthy and observant.

"When would you need an answer?" Cord asked.

Hayes smiled, and this time it reached his eyes. "I was hoping you'd ask that. How does right now sound?"

Cord looked at the badge again, thinking about his dwindling funds and the conversation he'd had with Pete the night before. The old liveryman had been right—this felt like legitimate government work, the kind of opportunity that didn't come along often for a man with his background.

"I'll take it," he said.

Hayes extended his hand across the table, and they shook on it. Then the Captain slid the wallet containing the badge across the table to Cord.

"Congratulations, Detective McBride. Welcome to territorial law enforcement."

The badge was heavier than Cord had expected, and the metal was cool against his palm. He pinned it to his vest, just inside his coat where it wouldn't be immediately visible but could be produced when needed.

"A few practical matters," Hayes said, pulling a thick envelope from his coat. "Here's your first month's pay, plus traveling expenses. You'll report your progress by telegraph when possible, and send written reports to this address in Denver." He handed Cord a card with an address printed in neat block letters. "If you need additional resources or run into trouble beyond your ability to handle, send word immediately."

Cord tucked the envelope and card into his coat pocket, trying not to think about how much money he was suddenly carrying. It felt strange to be on someone's payroll again after years of living from one odd job to the next.

"Any questions?" Hayes asked.

"Just one. You mentioned territorial interests, but you haven't said exactly which office you represent."

Hayes's expression didn't change, but something flickered behind his eyes—a momentary pause that was gone almost before Cord noticed it.

"I report directly to the territorial governor's office," Hayes said smoothly. "This rustling problem has reached the level where it requires special attention, and Governor Moonlight has given me broad authority to address it." He stood, indicating the meeting was over. "You should plan to leave for Fort Collins as soon as possible. Time is important in these matters."

Cord rose as well, extending his hand. "I won't let you down, Captain."

"I'm sure you won't. Good luck, Detective McBride."

Outside the Railroad House, Cord walked slowly back toward Pete's stable, his mind working over the conversation. Everything about Hayes had seemed legitimate—the bearing of a military man, the knowledge of territorial law enforcement, the professional way he'd handled the meeting. The badge felt real enough, and the money in his pocket was certainly genuine.

But something about the conversation nagged at him, though he couldn't put his finger on what it was. Maybe it was the way Hayes had deflected his question about which specific office he represented, or the slight pause before he'd mentioned Governor Moonlight. Or maybe it was just that after years of bad luck and disappointment, anything that seemed too good to be true probably was.

Pete was mucking out the stalls when Cord returned, and the old man looked up expectantly.

"How'd it go?"

Cord opened his coat to show the badge. "I'm now a territorial detective, assigned to investigate cattle rustling along the railroad line."

Pete leaned on his pitchfork and grinned. "Well, I'll be damned. Sixty dollars a month and all the trouble you can handle, I'd guess."

"Something like that." Cord pulled out the envelope Hayes had given him and counted out twenty dollars. "This should cover what I owe you for the winter, plus a little extra for the inconvenience."

Pete waved the money away. "Keep it, son. You'll need traveling money, and I've got everything I need right here."

"I insist." Cord pressed the bills into the old man's hand. "You took me in when I didn't have anywhere else to go. That's worth something."

"All right then, but you come back through Cheyenne, you've got a place to stay." Pete tucked the money into his shirt pocket. "When do you leave?"

"Today, if I can manage it. Need to get up to Fort Collins and start earning my keep."

"Fort Collins is good country. You'll like it up there." Pete resumed his work, then paused. "Just remember what I told you about this town, Cord. Things aren't always what they seem, and that goes double when there's big money involved."

Cord nodded, but his mind was already moving ahead to the journey north and the work waiting for him there. For the first time in years, he had a legitimate job with decent pay and the backing of proper authority. Whatever Pete's concerns about Cheyenne, Cord was confident he could handle whatever problems he might encounter as a territorial detective.

An hour later, he was riding north out of Cheyenne on a solid bay gelding he'd purchased from Pete, his few possessions packed in saddlebags and his new badge pinned securely inside his coat. The spring sun was warm on his back, and the road ahead stretched through rolling grassland toward the mountains.

For the first time since Little Bighorn, Cord McBride felt like he was exactly where he was supposed to be, doing exactly what he was meant to do. If there was trouble waiting for him in Fort Collins, he'd handle it the same way he'd handled everything else—one step at a time, and with his eyes wide open.

Behind him, the smoke from Cheyenne's locomotives rose into the clear Wyoming sky, and ahead lay whatever challenges came with wearing a badge in country where rustlers and honest ranchers might be harder to tell apart than a man might hope.

But that was tomorrow's problem. Today, he was Detective Cord McBride, and he had work to do.

Chapter 3: First Assignment

Fort Collins sat in a valley between rolling hills and the Front Range of the Rocky Mountains, a growing town that served the ranchers and farmers scattered across the northern Colorado Territory. The Cache la Poudre River ran alongside the main street, and cottonwoods lined its banks, their new spring leaves bright green against the brown landscape that was just beginning to shake off winter.

Cord rode into town in the late afternoon, his bay gelding picking its way carefully around the mud holes that marked the main thoroughfare. Fort Collins was smaller than Cheyenne but had the same sense of energy and growth—new buildings going up, wagons loaded with supplies heading out to distant homesteads, and the constant activity of a community that expected good times ahead.

The Western Union telegraph office occupied a narrow building sandwiched between a dry goods store and a barber shop. Through the front window, Cord could see the familiar setup—a wooden counter, telegraph key, and message forms scattered across a desk. What he hadn't expected was the woman working behind the counter.

Carmen Delgado was bent over a ledger, her dark hair pulled back in a practical bun that didn't quite conceal its thickness. She wore a simple white blouse and dark skirt, but there was something about the way she carried herself that suggested she was more than just a telegraph operator filling in until a man could take the job.

Cord tied his horse to the hitching post and pushed through the door, the bell above it announcing his arrival with a sharp chime.

She looked up from her work, and Cord found himself looking into dark eyes that were both intelligent and cautious. Her face was striking rather than conventionally pretty—high cheekbones and olive skin that spoke of mixed heritage, with a mouth that looked like it could smile easily but was currently set in a professional expression.

"Can I help you?" Her voice carried a slight accent, musical but controlled.

"I'm looking for Carmen Delgado. I believe she's expecting me."

Those dark eyes studied him more carefully, taking in the dust on his clothes, the way he wore his gun, and something else that Cord couldn't identify.

"And you are?"

"Cord McBride." He opened his coat far enough to show the badge pinned to his vest. "Territorial detective. Captain Hayes said you'd been keeping track of the rustling situation for him."

Recognition flickered across her features, followed immediately by something that might have been relief or concern—Cord couldn't tell which.

"Detective McBride. Yes, I've been expecting you." She moved to the front of the counter, and Cord noticed she was taller than he'd first thought, with the kind of grace that suggested she was comfortable in her own skin. "Captain Hayes sent word that you'd be coming to investigate the missing cattle."

"What can you tell me about it?"

Carmen glanced toward the front window, checking the street, then moved to flip the sign in the door from "Open" to "Closed."

"We should talk privately," she said. "There are things about this situation that are better discussed away from curious ears."

She led him through a curtained doorway into a back room that served as both her living quarters and office space. It was neat and simply furnished—a small table, two chairs, a narrow bed in one corner, and shelves lined with books and papers. A coffeepot sat on a small stove, and the room smelled faintly of coffee and the lavender soap she used.

"Sit, please," she said, gesturing toward one of the chairs while she poured coffee from the pot. "You've had a long ride from Cheyenne."

Cord accepted the cup gratefully, noticing that her hands were steady and capable. Everything about Carmen Delgado suggested competence, but there was an undercurrent of tension that made him think she was more involved in this situation than a simple informant might be.

"Captain Hayes said several ranchers in this area have lost cattle," he said.

"Three ranchers, to be precise." Carmen settled into the chair across from him, her own cup cradled in both hands. "Miguel Santos lost forty head two weeks ago. The Morrison ranch lost thirty head last week. And yesterday, Ben Kowalski rode into town saying someone had made off with his entire herd—nearly two hundred cattle."

Cord set down his coffee cup. Two hundred cattle was a substantial theft, the kind that suggested organization and planning rather than opportunistic rustling.

"Any witnesses? Tracks?"

"Santos found tracks leading east from his property, toward the Nebraska border. Morrison's cattle seemed to have been moved in the same direction." Carmen's dark eyes met his. "But here's what's strange—in each case, the rustlers only took certain animals. They left behind the older cattle, the ones that wouldn't travel well, and concentrated on young steers and breeding stock."

"Someone who knows cattle," Cord mused. "And knows what will bring the best price."

"Exactly. This isn't random theft by desperate men. It's organized, deliberate, and profitable." Carmen leaned forward slightly. "There's something else. In each case, the rustling happened just before the ranchers were planning to drive their cattle to market. Almost as if someone knew their schedules."

25

That was interesting. It suggested the rustlers had access to information about ranching operations, which meant they either had contacts in the community or were watching the ranches more carefully than anyone had realized.

"I'll need to talk to these ranchers," Cord said. "See the tracks for myself, get a better sense of what we're dealing with."

"I can arrange that. Santos and Morrison are both honest men who'll tell you what they know. Kowalski..." She hesitated. "Kowalski is more complicated."

"How so?"

"He's not well-liked in the community. Some people think he's too quick to make deals that benefit himself at the expense of his neighbors. But his cattle are still gone, and theft is theft."

Cord nodded. In his experience, victims weren't always sympathetic, but that didn't make them any less deserving of justice.

"What about local law enforcement? Sheriff been involved?"

Carmen's expression tightened slightly. "Sheriff Brennan is... limited in his capabilities. He's good enough for dealing with drunk cowboys and settling disputes over property lines, but this is beyond his experience. He's also not eager to chase rustlers into territory where he doesn't have jurisdiction."

"Meaning Nebraska, or meaning Indian territory?"

"Both. The tracks Santos found led east toward the Platte River. Beyond that, you're talking about dispute land, tribal territory, places where a local sheriff's authority doesn't carry much weight."

Cord had expected as much. Rustlers often operated along territorial boundaries precisely because it made pursuit more complicated. Local law enforcement was reluctant to chase criminals beyond their jurisdiction, and by the time word reached officials who could act, the trail was cold.

"I'll start with the Morrison ranch tomorrow," he said. "It's the most recent, so the tracks might still be clear enough to follow."

"I'll send word that you're coming." Carmen stood and moved to a small desk in the corner, pulling out paper and pen. "There's a good hotel on Main Street—the Colorado House. Clean rooms and decent food."

"What about you?" Cord asked. "Hayes mentioned you were keeping track of the situation for him. How long have you been working on this?"

Carmen's hand stilled for a moment, and when she looked up, there was something guarded in her expression.

"I've been the telegraph operator here for two years," she said carefully. "I hear things, see patterns in the messages that come through. When the rustling started getting worse, I began keeping notes, looking for connections."

It was a reasonable explanation, but Cord sensed there was more to it. Carmen Delgado struck him as someone who was used to keeping secrets, and he wondered what she wasn't telling him.

"Captain Hayes said you were reliable," he said. "That's good enough for me."

She smiled then, the first genuine smile he'd seen from her, and it transformed her face completely. For a moment, the professional mask dropped away, and he caught a glimpse of warmth and humor underneath.

"Thank you. I hope I can be helpful."

"I'm sure you will be." Cord stood, setting his empty coffee cup on the small table. "I should get settled at the hotel and let you get back to work."

Carmen walked him to the front door, flipping the sign back to "Open" as they passed through the main office.

"Detective McBride," she said as he reached for the door handle. "Be careful out there. These rustlers aren't random thieves looking for easy money. They're organized, they're smart, and they won't hesitate to use violence if they're cornered."

"I'll keep that in mind." Cord touched the brim of his hat. "Thank you for the coffee and the information."

"De nada." The Spanish slipped out naturally, and she seemed to realize it. "You're welcome."

Cord stepped out into the late afternoon sun, untied his horse, and led it down the street toward the Colorado House. As he walked, he found himself thinking about Carmen Delgado. She was clearly intelligent and observant, and her analysis of the rustling situation showed a keen understanding of criminal behavior. But there had been moments during their conversation when he'd sensed she was holding something back.

The hotel was as advertised—clean, comfortable, and reasonably priced. Cord got a room on the second floor with a view of the street, stabled his horse, and treated himself to his first restaurant meal in months. The beef was good, the potatoes were better, and the coffee was almost as good as what Carmen had served him.

As he ate, he listened to the conversations around him. Fort Collins was the kind of town where everyone knew everyone else's business, and it didn't take long to pick up useful information. The Morrison ranch was about five miles northeast of town. Santos had a smaller spread further east, closer to the river. And Ben Kowalski's place was the largest of the three, situated on good grazing land that bordered both territorial and tribal boundaries.

After dinner, Cord walked the main street, getting a feel for the town and the people. Fort Collins seemed prosperous and growing, with the kind of optimism that came from being in the right place at the right time. The railroad would reach here eventually, and when it did, the town would boom the same way Cheyenne had.

But underneath the optimism, he sensed the same tension he'd noticed in Cheyenne—the feeling that not everyone was playing by the same rules, and that some folks were getting rich while others struggled to hold onto what they had.

As he walked past the telegraph office, he noticed a light still burning in the back room. Carmen was working late, or perhaps she lived such a solitary life that evening and night blended together. He found himself wondering about her background, her family, and how a half-Mexican woman had ended up running a telegraph office in a Colorado Territory town.

Back at the hotel, Cord sat by his window and planned the next day's work. He'd start at the Morrison ranch, examine the tracks and the crime scene, then work his way east following whatever trail the rustlers had left. If Carmen was right about the direction they'd taken, he'd eventually find himself riding toward Nebraska and the disputed territories beyond.

It was exactly the kind of work he'd signed up for, and exactly the kind of challenge that made the badge in his vest feel worthwhile. For the first time since accepting Hayes's offer, Cord felt like he was earning his sixty dollars a month.

What he didn't know yet was that following those tracks east would lead him into country where territorial authority meant less than the ability to survive, and where the line between lawman and target could disappear as quickly as cattle in the night.

But that was tomorrow's problem. Tonight, he had a comfortable bed, a decent meal in his stomach, and the satisfaction of knowing he was finally doing work that mattered.

Outside his window, Fort Collins settled into evening quiet, while somewhere to the east, rustlers were probably planning their next raid and counting the profits from their last one.

Cord McBride intended to make sure those profits came at a much higher price than they expected.

Chapter 4: Trail of the Rustlers

The Morrison ranch sat in a shallow valley five miles northeast of Fort Collins, a modest spread with a frame house, a small barn, and several corrals that showed signs of recent construction. Tom Morrison met Cord at the gate, a weathered man in his fifties whose handshake was firm and whose eyes held the kind of wariness that came from losing livestock to thieves.

"Appreciate you coming out, Detective," Morrison said, leading Cord toward the pasture where the cattle had been taken. "Sheriff Brennan took a look, but he said tracking wasn't his strong suit."

"Tell me what happened," Cord said, dismounting and ground-tying his horse.

"Happened three nights ago. I had thirty head in this pasture—young steers I was planning to drive to Denver next week." Morrison pointed toward a fenced area near the creek. "Come morning, they were gone. No sign of a struggle, no dead cattle. Professional job."

Cord walked the fence line, looking for the kind of details that might tell him more about the thieves. The gate showed no signs of being forced, which meant the rustlers either had keys or knew enough about ranching to work the latch quietly in the dark.

"Any of your neighbors have problems with you?" Cord asked.

Morrison shook his head. "I get along with folks well enough. Pay my debts, mind my own business. These weren't neighbors, Detective. These were men who knew what they were doing."

The tracks were still visible in the soft earth near the creek —horses and cattle, heading east just as Carmen had said. Cord knelt beside the clearest hoofprints, studying the patterns. At least four horses, possibly five, and from the depth of the impressions, the riders were experienced enough not to push the cattle too hard.

"They took their time," he said, standing and brushing dirt from his hands. "No panic, no rush. Moved the herd at a pace that wouldn't stress the animals or leave obvious signs."

"That's what worries me," Morrison said. "Random thieves would have run those cattle hard, tried to get as far away as possible before anyone noticed they were missing. These men planned this."

Cord followed the trail east for nearly a mile before it reached harder ground where the tracks became more difficult to read. But the direction was clear enough— straight toward the Platte River and the disputed territories beyond.

"I'm going to follow this," he told Morrison. "See where it leads."

"You be careful, Detective. That's rough country east of here, and a man alone can find more trouble than he's looking for."

Cord spent the rest of the morning following the trail, reading sign and trying to build a picture of the men he was tracking. The rustlers had been careful but not obsessively so—they'd stayed to established cattle trails when possible, avoided soft ground that would hold clear tracks, and kept their stolen herd moving at a steady pace that wouldn't attract attention.

By noon, he was fifteen miles east of Fort Collins, in rolling grassland that stretched toward the South Platte River. The tracks were harder to follow here, but he'd learned enough about his quarry to make educated guesses about their route.

That was when he saw the dust cloud.

It was small and moving slowly, maybe two miles ahead—the kind of dust that came from a group of horsemen moving cattle at an easy pace. Cord reined in his bay and studied the landscape, looking for cover and the best approach.

A line of cottonwoods marked a creek running roughly parallel to the direction the dust cloud was moving. If he could get into those trees, he might be able to get close enough to see what he was dealing with before deciding on his next move.

Twenty minutes later, Cord was belly-down on a small rise overlooking a natural meadow where four men were resting a herd of cattle beside the creek. Even at a distance, he could see that the cattle carried different brands—exactly what he'd expect from a mixed herd of stolen livestock.

The rustlers had the relaxed attitude of men who didn't expect trouble. Two were watering their horses while a third dozed against his saddle. The fourth was examining the cattle, probably checking for injuries or signs of stress.

Professional, organized, and confident. Everything Carmen had suggested about this operation appeared to be true.

Cord studied the setup for several minutes, noting the positions of the men, their horses, and the natural features of the meadow that might provide cover or concealment. Then he worked his way back to his horse and began planning his approach.

The direct confrontation came an hour later, when the rustlers were pushing their stolen herd through a narrow gap between two hills. Cord had positioned himself on the high ground where he could cover the gap, and when the first rider came through, he called out in a voice that carried clearly in the still air.

"That's far enough! Territorial detective. I want to talk to you men."

The reaction was immediate and told him everything he needed to know about their guilt. The lead rider yanked his horse around, his hand dropping toward his gun, while the other three spread out in practiced positions that suggested they'd been in similar situations before.

"Easy," Cord called, his own hand resting casually on his gun butt but not drawing. "I just want to ask some questions about those cattle."

"Questions about what?" The lead rider was a lean man with a week's worth of stubble and the kind of eyes that never stopped moving. "We're just moving our herd to better grass."

"Interesting herd," Cord said, urging his horse down the slope until he was within easy talking distance. "Three different brands that I can see from here. Must have been some complicated business deals."

The rustlers exchanged glances, and Cord could see them weighing their options. They were armed and outnumbered him four to one, but they were also caught red-handed with stolen cattle, and killing a territorial detective would bring more heat than they probably wanted to deal with.

"Look, friend," the lean man said, trying a reasonable tone. "Maybe we can work something out here. No need for this to get complicated."

"I agree," Cord said. "Here's how we keep it simple. You boys ride away right now, leave the cattle, and I'll give you a ten-minute head start before I follow your tracks. Or we can do this the hard way, and somebody's going to get hurt."

It was a bluff, but a reasonable one. Cord was confident in his ability to handle himself in a fight, but four-to-one odds weren't something he wanted to test unless he had no choice.

The rustlers seemed to be thinking the same thing. The lean man looked at his companions, and Cord could see the silent communication that passed between experienced criminals weighing risk against profit.

"Those cattle are worth good money," one of the others said.

"Not as much as staying alive," Cord replied. "And not nearly as much as staying out of territorial prison."

The standoff lasted another thirty seconds before the lean man made his decision.

"Hell with it," he said. "There's always more cattle." He looked at Cord with something that might have been respect. "You've got sand, Detective. Hope it doesn't get you killed."

"I'll keep that in mind."

The rustlers rode away without looking back, leaving behind a herd of thirty-some cattle that Cord now had to figure out how to return to their rightful owners. It wasn't the most dramatic confrontation he'd ever been in, but it was satisfying in its own way—a clean resolution that put stolen property back where it belonged without anyone getting shot.

Of course, that left him with the practical problem of moving thirty head of cattle back toward Fort Collins by himself, but he'd faced worse challenges.

It took him the better part of two days to get the recovered cattle back to town, and by the time he arrived, word of his success had already spread through the community. Tom Morrison was there to claim his steers, grateful and effusive in his thanks. Miguel Santos identified another dozen head as belonging to him.

But it was the remaining cattle that presented Cord with his first real puzzle.

"Those aren't mine," Morrison said, looking at a group of six shorthorn steers that carried a brand Cord didn't recognize. "Never seen that brand before."

"Nor me," Santos agreed. "But they're good-looking animals. Whoever owns them, he knows cattle."

Carmen was waiting for Cord when he finally made it back to the telegraph office that evening, tired and dusty from two days of playing cowboy.

"I heard about your success," she said, pouring coffee without being asked. "The whole town's talking about it."

"Part of it, anyway." Cord accepted the coffee gratefully and settled into the chair that was already starting to feel familiar. "I recovered most of the stolen cattle, but there are some animals I can't identify. Brand I don't recognize, and nobody in town claims them."

Carmen's expression became thoughtful. "What does the brand look like?"

Cord described it as best he could, and Carmen made notes on a piece of paper.

"I can send some inquiries," she said. "Check with other telegraph offices, see if anyone recognizes the brand."

"Appreciate that." Cord studied her face in the lamplight. There was something different about her tonight—a tension that hadn't been there before, as if his success had raised new concerns rather than resolving old ones.

"Detective McBride," she said carefully. "In your experience, how often do you find that situations are exactly what they appear to be at first glance?"

It was an odd question, and the way she asked it suggested she had something specific in mind.

"Not often," he said honestly. "Most times, there's more going on underneath than shows on the surface. Why?"

Carmen was quiet for a moment, turning her coffee cup in her hands.

"These rustling cases," she said finally. "The pattern troubles me. Professional thieves, organized operations, cattle moved across territorial boundaries. It feels like more than simple theft."

"Meaning what?"

"I'm not sure yet. But I think you should be very careful about assuming that everyone who claims to own cattle actually does, and that everyone who appears to be stealing them actually is."

Before Cord could ask what she meant by that, Carmen stood and moved to the window, looking out at the darkening street.

"There are things about this situation that I haven't told you," she said without turning around. "Things I'm not sure I understand myself."

"Such as?"

"Such as the fact that some of the ranchers who've reported stolen cattle have been buying livestock from sources that might not be entirely legitimate themselves." She turned back to face him. "And such as the possibility that your Captain Hayes might not be representing exactly the interests he claims to represent."

The words hit Cord like cold water. "What are you saying?"

"I'm saying that before you recover any more 'stolen' cattle, you might want to make very sure they were actually stolen in the first place." Carmen's dark eyes were serious and worried. "And I'm saying that territorial law enforcement has some complicated politics that a honest man might not be aware of."

Cord set down his coffee cup and studied Carmen's face. She was clearly troubled by something, and her warnings had the ring of knowledge rather than speculation.

"Tell me what you know," he said.

Carmen was quiet for a long moment, then shook her head.

"Not yet. I need to be sure of my facts before I make accusations. But Detective McBride—Cord—please be careful. I think you may be an honest man caught in the middle of something that isn't honest at all."

That night, lying in his hotel room, Cord found himself thinking about Carmen's warnings and the unidentified cattle he'd recovered along with the obviously stolen ones. Was it possible that some of the "rustling" he was investigating was actually something else? And if so, what did that say about the people who had hired him?

For the first time since pinning on his badge, Cord McBride began to wonder if the authority he represented was as legitimate as he'd believed. And if it wasn't, then what exactly had he gotten himself into?

Tomorrow, he decided, he would start looking for answers to those questions. Even if he didn't like what he found.

Chapter 5: The Other Side

The telegram from Captain Hayes arrived three days after Cord's successful recovery of the stolen cattle, delivered by Carmen with an expression that suggested she'd read it and didn't like what it said.

"New assignment," she said, handing him the yellow paper. "Apparently your success has impressed someone."

Cord unfolded the telegram and read Hayes's precise handwriting: "REPORTS OF CATTLE THEFT NEAR STERLING STOP INVESTIGATE HOMESTEADER GUSTAV HOFFMAN STOP SUSPECTED OF HARBORING STOLEN LIVESTOCK STOP RECOVER PROPERTY AND ARREST IF NECESSARY STOP HAYES"

"Sterling's a long ride from here," Cord said, looking up from the message.

"Two days, maybe three if the weather turns." Carmen poured coffee for both of them, her movements precise but tense. "It's also close to the Nebraska border, in country where homesteaders and cattlemen don't always see eye to eye."

Cord studied the telegram again. Something about the wording bothered him, though he couldn't put his finger on what it was.

"You know anything about this Hoffman?"

Carmen was quiet for a moment, and when she spoke, her voice was carefully neutral.

"I know Gustav Hoffman filed on a homestead claim east of Sterling about two years ago. German immigrant, fought in the war, trying to build a life for his family." She paused. "I also know that some of the bigger ranchers in that area don't like homesteaders settling on what they consider open range."

"That's not unusual. But if he's harboring stolen cattle..."

"If he is." Carmen's emphasis on the word was slight but unmistakable. "Remember what I told you about being sure of your facts."

Cord folded the telegram and tucked it into his shirt pocket. Carmen's warnings from the other night still echoed in his mind, along with his own growing questions about the unidentified cattle he'd recovered.

"I'll ride out this morning," he said. "Should be back in a few days."

"Cord." Carmen's use of his first name made him look up sharply. "Be very careful who you trust out there. And remember that sometimes the line between victim and criminal isn't as clear as we'd like it to be."

The ride to Sterling took him through country that was slowly changing from the established ranching territory around Fort Collins to the newer, more contested lands where homesteaders were carving farms out of what had been open range. The further east he rode, the more evidence he saw of that conflict—abandoned homesteads with charred foundations, cattle with brands that had been recently changed, and the general air of tension that came from too many people wanting the same land for different purposes.

Sterling itself was a small town built around a railroad stop, serving both the established cattle ranches and the growing number of homesteads in the area. Cord arrived in the late afternoon and made his way to the local saloon, where the kind of information he needed was usually available for the price of a few drinks.

"Gustav Hoffman?" The bartender, a heavy-set man with German accent of his own, considered the question while polishing a glass. "Ja, I know Gustav. Good man. Works hard, minds his business."

"Heard he might be having some trouble with his neighbors."

The bartender's expression darkened slightly. "Depends on which neighbors you mean. Some folks around here think homesteaders got no business settling on range land, even when it's legal to do so."

"Any truth to the rumors about him keeping cattle that don't belong to him?"

"Truth?" The bartender set down his glass and leaned across the bar. "Truth is, Gustav bought those cattle fair and square from a man who needed quick money. Got the bill of sale and everything. But certain people don't like the idea of a homesteader owning good breeding stock."

That was interesting. Cord bought the man a drink and asked for directions to the Hoffman place.

The homestead sat on a section of good bottomland about five miles east of Sterling, with a modest frame house, a sturdy barn, and fenced pastures that showed the kind of careful attention that came from a man who understood that his land was his future. Smoke was rising from the chimney as Cord rode into the yard, and he could see a woman working in a kitchen garden beside the house.

Gustav Hoffman emerged from the barn as Cord dismounted—a big man in his forties with the broad shoulders and calloused hands of someone who did his own work. His face was weathered and serious, and his eyes held the wariness of a man who'd learned to be careful around strangers.

"Help you?" Hoffman's English was accented but clear.

"I'm Detective McBride, territorial law enforcement." Cord showed his badge. "I'd like to ask you some questions about your cattle."

Hoffman's expression didn't change, but Cord caught a quick glance toward the house where the woman had stopped working and was watching them with obvious concern.

"What about my cattle?"

"I've had reports that you might be keeping livestock that doesn't belong to you."

Now Hoffman's face did change, anger replacing wariness. "Who says this?"

"That doesn't matter. What matters is whether it's true."

45

For a moment, Cord thought the big German might refuse to answer. Then Hoffman nodded toward his barn.

"Come. I show you my cattle. I show you papers too."

The pasture behind the barn held about twenty head of mixed cattle—shorthorns, mostly, with a few longhorns mixed in. They were well-cared for and in good condition, the kind of small herd that a careful homesteader might build over time.

"These cattle," Hoffman said, "I buy from rancher named Peterson. He need quick money to pay debts, so he sell cheap. I got bill of sale, signed and witnessed."

"Can I see that bill of sale?"

Hoffman led him back to the house, where he introduced Cord to his wife Anna, a small, worried-looking woman who offered coffee while her husband rummaged through a wooden box of papers.

"Here," Hoffman said, producing a folded document. "Bill of sale for twenty head of cattle, sold by James Peterson of the Circle P Ranch to Gustav Hoffman. Signed, dated, witnessed."

Cord examined the paper carefully. It appeared legitimate —properly formatted, signed by both parties, and witnessed by someone with a legible signature. The date was three weeks old, and the price seemed reasonable for the quality of cattle he'd seen.

"This Peterson," Cord said. "He still around?"

"No. He sell his ranch after he sell me the cattle. Said he was going back east, maybe Ohio." Hoffman's expression was grim. "But before he go, he tell me some people might make trouble for me about these cattle. He say there are men who don't like homesteaders owning good stock."

"What kind of trouble?"

"People saying I steal cattle. People saying homesteaders got no business keeping breeding stock. People who want me to fail so they can buy my land cheap."

It was a story Cord had heard variations of throughout the territories—the conflict between established ranchers and newcomers, between those who saw land as something to be owned and those who saw it as something to be controlled. Usually, the law was clear enough to sort out legitimate ownership from theft.

But sitting in Gustav Hoffman's kitchen, looking at a bill of sale that appeared genuine and listening to a man who seemed honest, Cord found himself wondering if the law was being used as a weapon rather than a tool for justice.

"Detective McBride," Anna Hoffman said, speaking for the first time since introductions. "My husband is good man. He work hard, he pay his debts, he make no trouble for neighbors. Why someone want to say he steal cattle?"

It was a fair question, and one Cord didn't have a good answer for.

"Mr. Hoffman," he said finally, "you mind if I look around a little more? Check your brands, see if there's anything that might help me understand what's going on?"

"Look all you want," Hoffman said. "I got nothing to hide."

Cord spent an hour examining the Hoffman cattle, checking brands and looking for signs of recent alteration. What he found troubled him more than he cared to admit. The cattle were clearly well-cared for and showed no signs of being recently stolen or driven hard. More importantly, their brands matched the description on Peterson's bill of sale.

But those brands also matched the description of cattle reported stolen from a ranch near Cheyenne two months earlier.

That evening, back in Sterling, Cord sat in his hotel room trying to make sense of what he'd learned. Either Gustav Hoffman was an accomplished liar with expertly forged papers, or he was an honest homesteader caught in the middle of something more complicated than simple cattle theft.

The telegram he sent to Captain Hayes was brief: "INVESTIGATED HOFFMAN STOP APPEARS TO HAVE LEGITIMATE OWNERSHIP PAPERS STOP REQUEST CLARIFICATION ON ORIGINAL THEFT REPORTS STOP MCBRIDE"

Hayes's response came back within hours: "PAPERS LIKELY FORGED STOP PETERSON RANCH NEVER EXISTED STOP ARREST HOFFMAN AND RECOVER CATTLE IMMEDIATELY STOP HAYES"

Cord read the telegram three times, each reading making him more uncomfortable. If Hayes was right, then Hoffman was a skilled criminal who'd managed to fool him completely. But if Hayes was wrong—or lying—then Cord was being asked to arrest an innocent man and steal his cattle.

He walked to the telegraph office to send a reply, but found himself hesitating over what to write. Finally, he composed a message asking for more time to investigate, citing the need to verify facts before making an arrest.

Hayes's response was swift and unambiguous: "NO DELAY STOP ARREST HOFFMAN TOMORROW OR FACE DISCIPLINARY ACTION STOP HAYES"

That night, Cord lay awake staring at the ceiling and thinking about Carmen's warnings. Was it possible that he'd been hired not to investigate cattle theft, but to provide a legal cover for it? Was his badge being used to legitimize what was essentially organized rustling?

The next morning brought an answer he hadn't expected. A rider arrived at the hotel with a message from the actual territorial governor's office in Denver, responding to an inquiry Cord had sent days earlier about Captain Hayes and his authority.

The message was short and devastating: "NO RECORD OF CAPTAIN BENJAMIN HAYES IN TERRITORIAL LAW ENFORCEMENT STOP NO AUTHORITY GRANTED FOR SPECIAL DETECTIVE POSITIONS STOP ADVISE CAUTION STOP TERRITORIAL ATTORNEY GENERAL"

Cord read the message twice, then sat down heavily on his hotel room bed. The badge pinned inside his coat suddenly felt like a piece of worthless metal, and the authority he thought he represented was nothing more than an elaborate fraud.

But if Hayes wasn't working for territorial law enforcement, who was he working for? And what was the real purpose of the job Cord had been hired to do?

One thing was certain—he wasn't going to arrest Gustav Hoffman on the orders of a man who had no legal authority to give them. But that left him with the question of what he was going to do instead.

The answer came to him as he packed his saddlebags and prepared to leave Sterling. He was going to find out who Captain Hayes really worked for, and what they really wanted. And he was going to start by following the trail of those unidentified cattle he'd recovered, the ones that had belonged to neither Morrison nor Santos.

Because if Carmen was right about not everything being what it seemed, then the real story behind the rustling was probably bigger and more complicated than anyone had told him.

And Cord McBride intended to find out just how big and complicated it really was, even if it meant discovering that the badge he wore was nothing more than a license to commit the very crimes he thought he was supposed to prevent.

The ride back toward Fort Collins gave him time to think, and by the time he reached the Cache la Poudre River, he'd made his decision. He would continue his investigation, but on his own terms and with his own objectives. And the first thing he needed to do was have a long conversation with Carmen Delgado about what she really knew about Captain Hayes and the people he worked for.

Because if he was going to be caught in the middle of a conspiracy, he at least wanted to understand what side he was really on.

Chapter 6: Deeper into the Territory

The railroad right-of-way stretched east across the prairie like a scar across the landscape, twin rails gleaming in the morning sun and telegraph poles marching toward the horizon in perfect formation. Cord rode parallel to the tracks, keeping enough distance to avoid the work crews that were extending the line toward Nebraska, but close enough to follow the reports of missing cattle that had brought him into this disputed territory.

Three days had passed since his confrontation with Hayes about the Hoffman situation, three days of carefully worded telegrams and growing suspicion about his real employers. Hayes had been furious about Cord's refusal to arrest the homesteader, but had backed down when Cord threatened to contact Denver directly about his authority. Instead, Hayes had given him a new assignment—investigate reports of cattle theft from railroad work crews who were keeping livestock to feed the construction gangs.

It was plausible enough, but Cord had learned to be suspicious of assignments that sent him further from civilization and deeper into territory where territorial law was more theory than practice.

The land here was different from the settled country around Fort Collins—wider, emptier, with the kind of vast sky that made a man feel small and exposed. Rolling grassland stretched in every direction, broken by creek beds lined with cottonwoods and the occasional rocky outcrop that provided the only landmarks in an ocean of grass.

It was also Lakota territory, or had been until the treaties and wars that pushed the tribes further north and east. Now it was disputed land, claimed by the territorial government but still traveled by Native hunting parties and war bands who didn't recognize the authority of Washington bureaucrats.

Cord had been riding for most of the morning when he spotted the dust cloud on the northern horizon—a thin line against the blue sky that spoke of riders moving fast across the open prairie. He reined in his bay gelding and studied the approaching dust, counting horses and trying to gauge intentions from movement patterns.

Seven riders, maybe eight, moving in the disciplined formation that suggested either cavalry or warriors who knew their business. Given the location and the fact that there were no military patrols scheduled for this area, Cord was betting on the latter.

He had two choices: ride hard for the railroad construction camp about five miles ahead, or find cover and hope the riders passed without noticing him. The problem with the first option was that his horse was already tired from three days of travel, and running would mark him as either prey or an enemy. The problem with the second was that there wasn't much cover on the open prairie, and experienced plains warriors would spot him long before he could hide effectively.

So Cord did the third thing—the one that required either courage or stupidity, and he wasn't sure which. He dismounted, loosened his horse's girth, and waited.

The Lakota riders came over a low ridge about ten minutes later, their ponies moving with the easy grace of animals bred for the plains. They spotted Cord immediately and spread into a loose semicircle as they approached, rifles and bows ready but not overtly threatening.

The leader was a man about Cord's age, with the kind of bearing that came from natural authority rather than appointed rank. He wore traditional buckskin leggings and shirt, but his rifle was a modern Winchester and his horse was a fine paint gelding that showed careful breeding.

"You are far from the white man's towns," the leader said in English that carried only a slight accent. "This is not a safe place for one man alone."

"I'm tracking stolen cattle," Cord replied, keeping his hands visible and his tone respectful. "Railroad cattle. Someone's been taking livestock from the construction crews."

The Lakota leader studied him for a moment, then dismounted and walked closer. The other riders remained mounted but relaxed slightly, a sign that their leader didn't consider Cord an immediate threat.

"I am Thomas Running Bear," the man said. "And you are?"

"Cord McBride. Territorial detective." Cord showed his badge, wondering if it meant anything to the Lakota or if they would recognize it as worthless.

Running Bear examined the badge with interest but no apparent recognition of its illegitimate nature.

"Detective," he said thoughtfully. "Like the blue coats who come to investigate treaty violations and cattle theft from our lands."

"You've had trouble with stolen cattle too?"

Running Bear's expression darkened. "For two moons, someone has been taking horses and cattle from our herds. Good animals, taken by men who know their business. We track them, but the trails always lead to railroad camps or white settlements where we cannot follow without starting a war."

Cord felt pieces of a larger puzzle starting to fit together in his mind. "These thieves—did they take only certain animals? Leave the old or injured behind?"

"Yes. Like men who know what will bring good prices at market." Running Bear's eyes sharpened. "You have seen this before?"

"I have. And I'm starting to think the same people who are stealing from your herds are the ones taking from the railroad crews and the homesteaders."

"But who would steal from both white and Lakota? Such a man would have enemies on all sides."

"Someone who profits from keeping all sides fighting each other instead of looking for the real thieves," Cord said. The words came out before he'd fully formed the thought, but as soon as he said them, he knew they were true.

Running Bear was quiet for a moment, considering this. Then he gestured toward his men.

"We have been tracking the latest theft for two days. The trail leads toward the railroad. You wish to see?"

Following a Lakota war party deeper into disputed territory wasn't the smartest thing Cord had ever done, but it might be the only way to get answers to the questions that had been plaguing him since his encounter with Gustav Hoffman.

"Lead the way," he said.

They rode together across the prairie, seven Lakota warriors and one territorial detective who was beginning to question everything he thought he knew about his job. Running Bear proved to be good company, educated in mission schools but firmly rooted in traditional ways, with the kind of practical intelligence that came from surviving in a world where the old ways and new realities had to coexist.

"You fought in the war between the states," Running Bear said as they rode. It wasn't a question.

"I did. Seventh Cavalry."

"At the battle where Long Hair died?"

Cord's hands tightened on his reins. "Little Bighorn. Yes."

"You survived that fight. That makes you either very lucky or very skilled."

"Mostly lucky," Cord said, which wasn't entirely true but was all he wanted to say about it.

Running Bear nodded as if he understood there were some subjects that weren't meant for casual conversation.

The trail they were following led steadily southeast, toward the railroad construction camp that Cord had been planning to visit. The tracks were clear enough—a mixed herd of horses and cattle, driven by experienced riders who knew how to move livestock efficiently across open country.

"There," Running Bear said, pointing toward a line of smoke on the horizon. "The iron horse camp."

But as they got closer, it became clear that something was wrong. There was too much smoke, and it was the wrong color—black and oily, the kind that came from burning buildings rather than cook fires.

They crested a low hill and saw the railroad camp spread out below them—or what was left of it. The construction offices were burning, supply wagons were overturned, and scattered equipment lay abandoned across the site. But there were no bodies, and the destruction looked more like systematic looting than the aftermath of a battle.

"Your railroad friends had visitors," Running Bear observed.

They rode into the camp carefully, weapons ready, but found no signs of recent violence. The buildings had been emptied before they were burned, and the equipment that was missing was the valuable, portable kind that could be easily sold.

"This wasn't an Indian raid," Cord said, examining the scene.

"No. Indians would take horses and weapons, maybe food. They would not bother with surveying equipment and office supplies." Running Bear pointed toward tracks leading away from the camp. "And they would not drive stolen cattle in the same direction they drove stolen railroad property."

The tracks were clear enough—the same mixed herd they'd been following, now combined with evidence of loaded wagons heading southeast toward the Nebraska border.

"Someone used your stolen cattle as cover for robbing the railroad camp," Cord realized. "Made it look like an Indian raid while they cleaned out everything valuable."

"And tomorrow, the newspapers will say that Lakota warriors attacked the railroad camp and stole cattle," Running Bear said grimly. "More reason for the army to come into our territory, more excuse to break the treaties."

The pieces of the conspiracy were becoming clearer to Cord, and he didn't like the picture they were forming. Someone was orchestrating thefts from all sides— homesteaders, ranchers, railroad companies, and Native tribes—while making sure that each group blamed the others for their losses.

"Running Bear," he said, "what if I told you that the man who hired me to investigate these thefts might not be working for territorial law enforcement?"

The Lakota leader studied him carefully. "Then I would say you are beginning to understand the real war that is being fought in this territory. Not between white and red, or between rancher and homesteader, but between those who profit from conflict and those who suffer from it."

They spent another hour examining the destroyed camp, gathering evidence and trying to piece together exactly what had happened. The picture that emerged was of a carefully planned operation designed to look like something it wasn't—professional thieves using the cover of ethnic conflict to hide their real activities.

"I need to get back to Cheyenne," Cord said finally. "There are people I need to talk to, questions I need to ask."

"And we must take word to our people that the cattle thieves are not what they seem," Running Bear replied. "Perhaps it is time for all the victims of these thefts to stop fighting each other and start looking for their real enemies."

They parted company at the railroad tracks, the Lakota riders heading north toward their tribal lands while Cord turned west toward Cheyenne. But before they separated, Running Bear had one final observation.

"Detective McBride," he said, "in my experience, when a man discovers he has been lied to about small things, he should expect to find he has been lied to about large things as well. Be careful who you trust."

The ride back to Cheyenne gave Cord plenty of time to think about Running Bear's warning and the evidence he'd gathered in the destroyed railroad camp. By the time he reached the outskirts of the city, he was convinced that the cattle rustling he'd been hired to investigate was just the visible edge of something much larger and more dangerous.

Someone was using ethnic tensions and territorial conflicts to hide a systematic campaign of theft that targeted everyone equally. And that someone had enough resources and connections to hire fake territorial detectives, forge official documents, and coordinate operations across hundreds of miles of frontier territory.

The question was who had that kind of power and organization, and what their ultimate goal might be. Cord had a growing suspicion that the answers to those questions would lead him back to Captain Hayes and the mysterious employers who had given him his worthless badge.

But first, he needed to talk to Carmen Delgado. Because if Running Bear was right about not trusting anyone, then Carmen was either his best ally in unraveling this conspiracy, or the person who was playing him more skillfully than anyone else.

And after three weeks of following false leads and chasing shadows, Cord McBride was ready to start demanding some real answers, regardless of what those answers might cost him.

Chapter 7: Questions and Passion

The lights of Cheyenne glowed against the evening sky as Cord rode back into town after five days in the disputed territories. His horse was tired, his clothes were dusty, and his mind was full of questions that seemed to multiply faster than he could find answers for them.

The livery stable was already closed for the night, so Cord put his bay up at the public corral behind the Railroad House and made his way through the quiet streets toward Fort Collins and Carmen. He needed to talk to someone he could trust, and despite Running Bear's warnings about trusting anyone, Carmen Delgado was the only person who had consistently told him truths he didn't want to hear.

The telegraph office was dark, but Cord could see a faint light in the back room window. He knocked softly on the rear door, and after a moment heard footsteps approaching.

"Cord?" Carmen's voice was cautious through the door.

"It's me."

The door opened, and Carmen stood silhouetted against the lamplight, wearing a simple cotton nightgown with a shawl wrapped around her shoulders. Her dark hair was loose around her face, and her eyes held a mixture of relief and worry that told him she'd been concerned about his absence.

"I was beginning to wonder if you were coming back," she said, stepping aside to let him in.

"So was I, for a while." Cord removed his hat and set it on the small table. "I need to talk to you, Carmen. About Hayes, about this job, about what's really going on out there."

Carmen studied his face in the lamplight, and whatever she saw there made her expression grow serious.

"You look like a man who's seen things that troubled him," she said. "Sit. I'll make coffee."

But as she moved toward the stove, Cord caught her arm gently, stopping her. The touch was meant to be casual, but the moment his hand made contact with her warm skin, something electric passed between them. Carmen looked up into his eyes, and Cord saw his own confused desire reflected there.

"The coffee can wait," he said softly.

Carmen's breath caught slightly. "Cord..."

"I know. This complicates things." His hand moved from her arm to cup her face, his thumb tracing the line of her cheekbone. "But everything else in my life has become so damned complicated that maybe one honest thing would be a blessing."

Carmen leaned into his touch for a moment, her eyes closing. Then she pulled back slightly, though she didn't move away from him.

"Honest," she repeated. "That's what you think this would be?"

"Isn't it?"

Carmen was quiet for a moment, studying his face. "There are things about me you don't know, Cord. Things I can't tell you, not yet."

"Are you married?"

"No."

"Are you working for Hayes?"

"Not the way you mean." Carmen's dark eyes were troubled. "But I'm not... I can't be completely honest with you about everything. Not yet."

Cord felt a familiar stab of disappointment, the same feeling he'd experienced when he'd discovered his badge was worthless. But looking into Carmen's eyes, he also saw something that gave him hope—genuine care, and what looked like pain at having to keep secrets.

"Then tell me what you can," he said. "And let me decide if it's enough."

Carmen was quiet for a long moment, her hand coming up to cover his where it still rested against her cheek.

"I can tell you that everything you're beginning to suspect about Hayes and your job is probably true," she said finally. "I can tell you that you're not the first man they've hired to do this kind of work, and the others... it didn't end well for them."

"What happened to them?"

"Some disappeared. Others had accidents. One was found shot in the back, supposedly by rustlers." Carmen's voice was steady, but Cord could see the fear in her eyes. "They all had one thing in common—they started asking too many questions."

The implications of what she was saying hit Cord like cold water. "You're saying Hayes has his previous detectives killed?"

"I'm saying that men who become inconvenient to Hayes's employers have a tendency to meet unfortunate ends." Carmen's hand tightened on his. "And I'm terrified that you're heading down the same path."

Cord absorbed this information, adding it to everything he'd learned in his conversation with Thomas Running Bear. The pattern was becoming clearer, and it was darker than he'd imagined.

"Carmen," he said, "how do you know all this?"

She was quiet for so long that he thought she wasn't going to answer. When she finally spoke, her voice was barely above a whisper.

"Because I've been watching. Waiting. Gathering information and looking for someone who might be strong enough and honest enough to help me stop them."

"Stop who?"

"The people Hayes works for. The people who are using ethnic conflicts and territorial disputes to hide the biggest theft operation the territories have ever seen." Carmen's eyes met his. "And I think... I hope... that you might be that person."

Before Cord could respond, Carmen rose on her tiptoes and kissed him, a soft, desperate kiss that tasted of coffee and fear and something that might have been hope. Cord's arms came around her, pulling her against him as the kiss deepened, and for a moment the questions and complications faded away, leaving only the warmth of human connection in a world that had become cold and dangerous.

When they finally broke apart, both were breathing hard, and Cord could see his own conflicted emotions reflected in Carmen's dark eyes.

"This is dangerous," she whispered. "For both of us."

"Everything's dangerous now," Cord replied. "At least this feels real."

Carmen smiled, a small, sad smile that broke his heart a little. "Real. Yes, this is real."

She led him to the narrow bed in the corner of her small room, and they came together with the kind of desperate passion that comes from two people who have found something precious in the middle of a world that seemed determined to take everything away from them. They made love slowly, carefully, as if memorizing each touch against the possibility that it might be the last time.

Afterward, they lay together in the lamplight, Carmen's head on Cord's chest, his fingers tracing patterns in her dark hair. The physical intimacy had only intensified the emotional connection between them, but it had also sharpened the edge of the secrets that still lay between them.

"Tell me about the others," Cord said quietly. "The detectives who came before me."

Carmen was quiet for a moment, her finger tracing the scar on his shoulder that he'd earned in a cavalry skirmish years before.

"The first was a man named Collins. Former army, like you. Hired six months ago to investigate rustling along the Colorado-Nebraska border." Her voice was carefully controlled. "He lasted three weeks before he started questioning his assignments. Found shot two days after he sent a telegram to Denver asking about Hayes's authority."

"And the others?"

"Stevens disappeared entirely. Just rode out one morning and never came back. His horse was found a week later, but no body." Carmen's finger stilled on his chest. "Morrison—not the rancher, a different Morrison—fell off his horse and broke his neck. Except he was an experienced rider who'd survived ten years of Indian fighting."

Three men, three convenient deaths. Cord was starting to understand why Carmen had been so worried about him.

"How do you know all this?"

"Because I've been keeping track. Because someone needs to remember these men and what happened to them."

Carmen lifted her head to look at him. "And because I've been waiting for someone who might be different."

"Different how?"

"Harder to kill. Smarter about staying alive. Too stubborn to quit when things get dangerous." Carmen's smile was soft but worried. "You survived Little Bighorn when everyone else in your unit died. That tells me something about your ability to stay alive when the odds are against you."

It was the second time someone had referenced his survival of that battle, and Cord was beginning to understand that his reputation was both an asset and a liability in this situation.

"Carmen," he said, "what exactly do you think I can do that the others couldn't?"

"Survive long enough to gather real evidence. Find out who's really behind this operation. Maybe even live to testify against them." Her dark eyes were serious. "But only if you're very, very careful about who you trust and what you do next."

Before Cord could respond, Carmen's expression changed, her head lifting as she listened to something he couldn't hear.

"Someone's coming," she whispered.

Cord heard it then—footsteps on the wooden sidewalk outside, moving with purpose toward the telegraph office. Carmen was already moving, pulling on her nightgown and shawl while Cord reached for his gun belt.

The knock on the front door was firm and official. "Miss Delgado! Telegraph for you!"

Carmen and Cord exchanged glances. Telegrams delivered at midnight were either emergencies or traps, and given everything they'd been discussing, neither option was particularly comforting.

"Coming!" Carmen called, then whispered to Cord, "Stay here. If this goes wrong, get out through the back."

She made her way to the front office, and Cord heard the sound of the door opening and muffled conversation. After a few minutes, she returned with a yellow telegraph form, her face pale in the lamplight.

"What is it?" Cord asked, though he suspected he already knew.

Carmen handed him the telegram. It was addressed to her but clearly meant for him: "MCBRIDE RETURN CHEYENNE IMMEDIATELY STOP NEW ASSIGNMENT URGENT STOP REPORT TO RAILROAD HOUSE TOMORROW MORNING STOP HAYES"

"He knows you're here," Carmen said quietly.

"Probably knows more than that." Cord crumpled the telegram. "Question is, what does he want me to do next?"

Carmen's expression was troubled. "Whatever it is, it will be designed to keep you busy and distracted while they finish whatever they're really planning."

"Or to put me in a position where I can have a convenient accident."

Carmen nodded grimly. "That too."

Cord got dressed, his mind working over the implications of Hayes's message. The timing wasn't accidental—Hayes had waited until he returned from the disputed territories, probably already knew what he'd found there, and was now moving to control the situation.

"I have to go back to Cheyenne," he said. "See what Hayes wants, try to learn more about his real employers."

"I know." Carmen helped him buckle his gun belt. "But Cord, promise me you'll be careful. Don't trust anything Hayes tells you, don't go anywhere alone if you can help it, and don't take any assignments that send you too far from help."

"What about you? If Hayes knows I was here..."

"I can take care of myself," Carmen said, though her voice carried a note of uncertainty. "I've been playing this game longer than you have."

Cord kissed her one more time, a gentle kiss that tasted of promise and fear in equal measure.

"This isn't over," he said.

"I hope not," Carmen replied. "But if something happens to you..."

"It won't." Cord's voice carried more confidence than he felt. "I'm too stubborn to die, remember?"

Carmen smiled, but the worry never left her eyes. "Just remember what I told you about trust. And remember that the people Hayes works for have resources you can't imagine and no scruples about using them."

As Cord made his way through the darkened streets back to his hotel, he found himself thinking about everything Carmen had told him. Three previous detectives, all dead or missing. A conspiracy that reached beyond simple cattle rustling into organized theft and systematic manipulation of territorial conflicts. And somewhere at the center of it all, the mysterious employers who had given Hayes the resources to hire fake detectives and orchestrate operations across hundreds of miles of frontier.

Tomorrow he would face Hayes again, but this time he would be asking different questions and looking for different answers. Because if Carmen was right about the fate of his predecessors, then his survival depended on learning the truth about who he was really working for and what they ultimately wanted.

The only question was whether he could learn that truth before they decided he knew too much to live.

Chapter 8: The Pattern Emerges

The Railroad House dining room was nearly empty at eight in the morning, with only a few railroad executives and territorial officials scattered among the elegant tables. Cord sat across from Captain Hayes, watching the man cut his steak with surgical precision while discussing the new assignment as if they were talking about the weather.

"Homesteaders near Sterling have been particularly troublesome," Hayes was saying, his pale blue eyes never quite meeting Cord's. "Reports of organized rustling, possibly coordinated with hostile Indians. The territorial government is very concerned."

Cord sipped his coffee and studied Hayes's face, looking for tells he might have missed in their previous meetings. Now that he knew the man was a fraud, certain details became more obvious—the way he deflected specific questions about his authority, the vague references to "territorial interests," the careful way he spoke about his employers.

"Which homesteaders specifically?" Cord asked.

Hayes consulted a leather portfolio beside his plate. "The Kowalski place, which you're already familiar with. The new Swedish settlement north of Sterling. And there are reports of problems with some of the German families who've been filing claims along Crow Creek."

All small operators. All people trying to build something from nothing. Cord thought about Gustav Hoffman and his legitimate bill of sale, about the way Hayes had insisted on his arrest despite clear evidence of proper ownership.

"What about the big operations?" Cord asked casually. "Any problems with the established ranches?"

"The large ranchers have the resources to protect themselves," Hayes replied smoothly. "It's the smaller operations that are vulnerable to organized theft. That's why territorial law enforcement is focusing its efforts there."

It was a reasonable explanation, but combined with everything Cord had learned over the past few days, it felt like another lie wrapped in plausible logic.

"Captain," Cord said, leaning forward slightly, "in the time I've been working for you, every assignment has targeted small ranchers, homesteaders, or railroad work crews. Never once have you sent me to investigate theft from one of the big cattle operations. Don't you find that curious?"

Hayes's knife paused for just a moment before resuming its careful cutting. "Not particularly. As I said, the large operations can take care of themselves."

"Or maybe they're not being targeted because they're part of whatever's really going on here."

Now Hayes did look up, his pale eyes sharp and calculating. "That's a serious accusation, Detective McBride. Do you have evidence to support it?"

"I have Gustav Hoffman's bill of sale. I have testimony from Thomas Running Bear about systematic theft from Lakota herds. I have a burned railroad camp that was made to look like an Indian raid." Cord kept his voice level and professional. ' And I have three dead detectives who preceded me in this job."

Hayes set down his knife and fork with deliberate care. "I'm not sure what you think you've discovered, but I assure you that territorial law enforcement takes its responsibilities seriously. If you have concerns about your assignments..."

"My concerns are about the authority behind those assignments," Cord interrupted. "I contacted Denver, Captain. The territorial attorney general's office has no record of you or any special detective program."

For a moment, Hayes's mask slipped, and Cord saw something cold and dangerous flicker behind his eyes. Then the professional facade returned, but it was thinner now, more obviously artificial.

"There are aspects of territorial security that aren't widely publicized," Hayes said carefully. "Certain operations require discretion and deniability."

"Whose operations, Captain? Who do you really work for?"

Hayes was quiet for a long moment, studying Cord's face. When he spoke, his voice had lost its official tone and taken on something that sounded almost conversational.

"You know, McBride, I warned my employers that hiring a Little Bighorn survivor might be a mistake. Men who've been through that kind of experience tend to be... resilient. Hard to discourage when they get an idea in their heads."

"Answer the question."

"I work for people who understand that the territories are changing, and that change requires management. The old ways—individual ranchers, small homesteaders, tribal hunting grounds—they're not efficient. They're not profitable." Hayes picked up his coffee cup. "Progress requires consolidation, and consolidation sometimes requires... encouragement."

Cord felt pieces of the puzzle clicking into place in his mind. "You're talking about forcing small operators off their land."

"I'm talking about natural economic forces, guided by people with the vision and resources to make the territories profitable for everyone." Hayes's smile was thin and cold. "Your job has been to provide legal justification for that process."

"By branding honest homesteaders as cattle thieves."

"By investigating legitimate complaints about livestock theft and taking appropriate action." Hayes's tone suggested he actually believed his own rationalization. "If some of those investigations result in failed homesteads or abandoned claims, that's simply the market working efficiently."

Cord thought about Gustav Hoffman, about the fear in his wife's eyes, about Thomas Running Bear's description of systematic theft from both sides of the territorial divide.

"And the actual rustling? The organized theft that's been hitting ranchers, homesteaders, and Indian tribes?"

"Necessary to maintain the fiction that there's a real problem requiring territorial intervention." Hayes finished his coffee. "Though I suspect you've already figured that out."

The casual admission hit Cord like a physical blow. Hayes was describing a conspiracy to steal from everyone while using territorial law enforcement as cover for driving small operators off their land.

"Who's behind it?" Cord asked quietly.

Hayes stood, leaving money on the table for his breakfast. "People with more power and resources than you can imagine, Detective. People who don't appreciate interference from idealistic former cavalrymen with overdeveloped consciences."

"That sounds like a threat."

"It's a statement of fact." Hayes adjusted his coat. "You have a choice to make, McBride. You can continue working for us, following orders and asking fewer questions, or you can find yourself experiencing the same kind of misfortune that befell your predecessors."

Hayes walked away, leaving Cord alone at the table with his coffee and the full realization of what he'd gotten himself into. He wasn't a territorial detective investigating cattle rustling—he was an unwitting enforcer for some kind of corporate conspiracy designed to consolidate control over territorial land and resources.

And based on Hayes's parting words, the people behind it were prepared to kill him if he didn't cooperate.

Cord finished his coffee, his mind working over everything he'd learned. The pattern was clear now: every assignment had been designed to target small operators who stood in the way of larger interests. Gustav Hoffman's cattle weren't stolen—they were legitimate property that someone wanted to use as an excuse to drive him off valuable land. The railroad camp hadn't been raided by Indians—it had been robbed by the same organization that employed Hayes, with the theft disguised as ethnic conflict.

Even his encounter with the rustlers who'd stolen Morrison's cattle took on a different meaning. Those men hadn't been random thieves—they'd been part of the same operation, probably hired to steal specific cattle that could then be "recovered" by territorial law enforcement, creating the appearance of effective policing while actually serving corporate interests.

As he walked back toward his hotel, Cord found himself thinking about Carmen's warnings and her hints that she'd been gathering information about Hayes and his employers. If she knew who was really behind the conspiracy, then she might also know how to stop them.

But first, he had to survive long enough to learn the truth and figure out what to do with it.

The streets of Cheyenne looked different to him now—not the bustling frontier town he'd first seen, but a stage set for a drama in which he'd been playing a role without understanding the script. The cattle pens, the railroad yards, the businessmen in their fine clothes—all of it took on a more sinister cast when viewed through the lens of organized conspiracy.

Back in his hotel room, Cord sat on the bed and took stock of his situation. He had a worthless badge, a dangerous employer, and knowledge that made him a threat to people with the resources to make him disappear. On the positive side, he had Carmen as a potential ally, and he'd begun to understand the scope of what he was up against.

The question was what to do next. Hayes had made it clear that Cord's choices were limited: cooperate or die. But there might be a third option—one that involved exposing the conspiracy and bringing its architects to justice.

It would be dangerous, probably suicidal, and would require resources and allies he wasn't sure he could find. But it was the only choice that allowed him to live with himself, and after nine years of drifting and trying to avoid other people's troubles, Cord McBride was finally ready to take a stand for something that mattered.

He strapped on his gun belt, checked his supplies, and prepared to ride back to Fort Collins. Carmen had promised to tell him more when she was certain of her facts, and now that he understood the stakes, it was time to hear everything she knew.

Because if he was going to fight back against Hayes and his employers, he was going to need all the help he could get. And he had the uncomfortable feeling that time was running out faster than any of them realized.

The war for the territories was being fought not with guns and cavalry, but with forged documents and manufactured crimes. And Cord had just discovered that he'd been fighting on the wrong side.

Now it was time to change sides, regardless of the consequences.

Chapter 9: The Puppet Master Revealed

The morning sun cast long shadows across Cheyenne's dusty streets as Cord made his way to the territorial records office. Hayes's words from the night before echoed in his mind like a funeral bell: *We clear out the small operators for the big interests.* Sleep had been impossible, his thoughts churning through every job he'd taken, every man he'd tracked down, every "rustler" he'd brought to justice.

The records clerk, a thin man with ink-stained fingers, looked up nervously as Cord approached. Word traveled fast in a territorial capital, and everyone knew about the incident at the Silver Dollar.

"I need to see the brand registrations for the past two years," Cord said, keeping his voice level. "And the shipping records from the Union Pacific cattle pens."

"That's... that's quite a lot of paperwork, Marshal. Might I ask what you're looking for?"

Cord fixed him with a steady stare. "Justice."

The clerk swallowed hard and began pulling ledgers from the shelves behind him. Cord settled at a corner table and opened the first volume, running his finger down columns of names, dates, and brand descriptions. What he found made his stomach turn.

James Mitchell, the small rancher from his first assignment—his Lazy M brand had been registered to one

"Samuel Michaels" just three days after Mitchell's arrest. The brand looked identical, except for a subtle addition that turned the M into what could be interpreted as an H with a connecting line.

The Heinrich family's Circle H brand had been similarly appropriated, registered under "Henry Holdings" the week Heinrich was charged with theft of his own cattle. Each case followed the same pattern: arrest the small rancher, appropriate the brand with minor alterations, claim the cattle as legally owned.

But who was behind these new registrations? The names meant nothing to him—obvious fronts, shell companies designed to obscure true ownership. Cord made careful notes in his leather journal, copying down dates, names, and brand descriptions. The pattern was unmistakable, but he needed to know who was pulling the strings.

"Afternoon, Marshal."

Cord looked up to find Carmen Torres approaching his table, her dark eyes reflecting the same wariness he'd seen in everyone since the saloon confrontation. She wore a simple blue dress, her hair pinned up neatly, every inch the respectable telegraph operator. But something in her expression suggested she knew more than she let on.

"Miss Torres." He gestured to an empty chair. "I was hoping I might run into you."

She sat carefully, glancing around the records office to ensure they weren't overheard. "I heard about your... disagreement with Mr. Hayes last night."

"Word travels fast."

"In a town this size, everything travels fast." She leaned forward, lowering her voice. "Including some information you might find interesting."

Cord set down his pen. "Such as?"

Carmen glanced toward the clerk, who was busy reorganizing files at the far end of the office. "The telegraph messages I've been handling lately. Mr. Hayes sends quite a few to someone in Denver. Someone with considerable influence in the cattle business."

"Go on."

"Silas Blackwood," she said quietly. "Ever heard of him?"

The name hit Cord like a physical blow. Silas Blackwood —everyone in the cattle trade knew that name. One of the largest operators in Colorado Territory, with holdings stretching into Wyoming. The man commanded respect in Denver's business circles, owned significant interests in several banks, and was rumored to have the ear of territorial officials.

"I know the name," Cord said carefully.

"Mr. Hayes works for him. All those jobs you've been taking—they're not random. Every small rancher you've gone after, every 'rustler' you've tracked down, they all had something Blackwood wanted. Usually land, sometimes cattle, often both."

Cord felt the ground shifting beneath him again, the same sensation he'd experienced when Hayes revealed the truth about territorial law enforcement. "How do you know this?"

Carmen's expression grew guarded. "I read the telegrams, Marshal. It's part of my job. And Mr. Hayes isn't particularly careful about what he says in his communications."

From her reticule, she produced a folded piece of paper. "I took the liberty of copying one of his more recent messages."

Cord unfolded the paper and read:

BLACKWOOD DENVER STOP TERRITORY CLEARED LARAMIE VALLEY STOP MITCHELL HEINRICH HOFFMAN OPERATIONS ELIMINATED STOP BRANDS TRANSFERRED STOP SHIPPING ROUTES SECURED STOP AWAITING FURTHER INSTRUCTIONS STOP HAYES

The words swam before Cord's eyes. Territory cleared. Operations eliminated. He thought of James Mitchell's wife, crying as her husband was led away in chains. Of the Heinrich children, watching their father branded a thief and a liar. Of Gustav Hoffman's weathered face, the confusion and hurt in his eyes.

"How many?" he asked quietly.

"How many what?"

"How many families have I destroyed for Silas Blackwood?"

83

Carmen's voice was gentle but firm. "Seventeen ranches in the past fourteen months. Small operators, most of them. Some homesteaders trying to build up herds. A few Mexican families with old Spanish land grants." She paused. "All of them standing in the way of Blackwood's expansion plans."

Cord closed his eyes, seeing the faces of the men he'd tracked, the families he'd left behind. Seventeen families. Seventeen lives destroyed because he'd been too trusting, too willing to believe in the rightness of his cause.

"The cattle I recovered," he said. "The stolen herds I returned to their 'rightful owners'..."

"Delivered to Blackwood's operation outside Denver. Rebranded, documented as legitimate purchases, then shipped east on the Union Pacific at preferential rates." Carmen's voice carried a note of something—anger, perhaps, or sympathy. "You've been very efficient, Marshal. Blackwood's operation has grown by over three thousand head in the past year, most of it through your efforts."

Cord opened his eyes and looked at her. Really looked at her. The careful way she held herself, the intelligence in her dark eyes, the fact that she somehow had access to information most people wouldn't think to look for.

"Who are you really?" he asked.

For a moment, she didn't answer. Then: "Someone who's been watching this operation from the inside, hoping someone with your... capabilities... might eventually see the truth."

"You've been using me."

"No more than Blackwood has been using you. The difference is, I wanted you to discover the truth. He wanted you to remain ignorant."

Cord looked down at the ledgers spread before him, at the copied telegram in his hands, at the evidence of his own unwitting complicity in a massive fraud. The weight of it settled on his shoulders like a lead blanket.

"What does Blackwood want with all this land?" he asked.

"Control," Carmen said simply. "The Union Pacific needs cattle for the eastern markets, and they want reliable suppliers who can guarantee large shipments on schedule. Small ranchers can't provide that kind of volume or consistency. But a large operation like Blackwood's can."

"So they eliminate the competition."

"Under color of law. Using territorial marshals with sterling reputations for honesty and efficiency." Her eyes met his. "Men like you."

The irony was bitter as alkali water. His reputation for integrity had made him the perfect tool for corruption. His skill at tracking had enabled theft on a massive scale. His determination to see justice done had perverted justice itself.

"The territorial government must know," he said.

"Some do. Others are simply bought. And some, I suspect, genuinely believe they're supporting legitimate business development." Carmen leaned back in her chair. "It's a very sophisticated operation, Marshal. Blackwood didn't build his empire by being careless or obvious."

Cord gathered up the ledgers and his notes. Seventeen families. Three thousand head of cattle. Hundreds of thousands of acres of prime grazing land. All of it orchestrated through a network of corruption that stretched from territorial officials to railroad executives to federal marshals.

"What happens now?" he asked.

Carmen stood, smoothing down her skirt. "That depends on you. You could still walk away. Take Hayes's offer, collect your money, and find somewhere else to make a living. Blackwood's operation is large enough that one more marshal won't make much difference."

"Or?"

"Or you could do what you've always done. Track down the thieves and bring them to justice." She paused at his look of confusion. "The real thieves, Marshal. The ones who've been stealing from seventeen families and calling it law enforcement."

She turned to leave, then stopped. "There's a café two blocks south of the telegraph office. If you decide you want to know more about Silas Blackwood's operation—the full extent of it—meet me there tonight at eight o'clock."

Cord watched her walk away, her footsteps echoing in the quiet records office. Then he looked down at the evidence spread before him: the ledgers showing fraudulent brand registrations, the telegram revealing the coordination between Hayes and Blackwood, his own notes documenting the systematic destruction of small ranching operations.

For fourteen months, he'd believed he was upholding the law. Instead, he'd been the instrument of its corruption.

The clerk approached hesitantly. "Will you be needing anything else, Marshal?"

Cord closed the last ledger and stood. "Just one thing. The name of whoever's been registering all these new brands for the past year. The real names, not the front companies."

The clerk's face went pale. "I... I'm not sure I understand."

"Samuel Michaels, Henry Holdings, all these convenient new cattle operations that seem to spring up right after small ranchers get arrested." Cord's voice carried the edge he usually reserved for dangerous men resisting arrest. "Who's really behind them?"

The man's hands shook as he reached for another ledger. "The... the registrations all came through the same law firm. Whitman and Associates out of Denver. They handle most of Mr. Blackwood's territorial business."

There it was. The final piece of the immediate puzzle. Silas Blackwood wasn't just buying up the cattle and land —he was doing it through legal channels, using his own attorneys to file the paperwork that made theft look like legitimate business.

Cord tucked his notes into his jacket and headed for the door. Behind him, he could hear the clerk fumbling with papers, probably preparing to send word to someone about the marshal's sudden interest in brand registrations and shipping records.

Let them know he was asking questions. Let them worry about what he might find next.

Outside, the afternoon sun beat down on Cheyenne's dusty streets, but Cord felt cold inside. Seventeen families. The number kept echoing in his mind as he walked toward his hotel. Seventeen families destroyed so that one man could build an empire, and he'd been the weapon Blackwood had used to do it.

But weapons could be turned on their wielders.

Tonight, he'd learn just how deep this corruption ran. And then he'd decide whether Silas Blackwood had enough money to buy his way out of justice.

The hunter had become the prey for too long. It was time to remember which role suited him better.

Chapter 10: The Railroad Connection

The Union Pacific cattle pens sprawled across ten acres on the eastern edge of Cheyenne, a maze of wooden corrals and loading chutes that funneled Wyoming beef toward the hungry markets of Chicago and New York. Cord had been there dozens of times before, usually to oversee the loading of recovered cattle bound for their rightful owners. Now, as he walked between the pens in the early morning light, he saw the operation with different eyes.

Carmen had suggested they meet here after their conversation at the café the night before. She'd promised to show him proof of the railroad's involvement in Blackwood's scheme, and Cord was beginning to understand that her knowledge of the conspiracy went deeper than a telegraph operator should reasonably possess.

"Over here," she called softly from behind a stack of shipping crates near the main office building.

Cord made his way through the maze of cattle pens, noting the brands on the animals waiting for shipment. Mixed herds, which was normal enough, but something nagged at him about the combination of marks. Too many similar brands, too many that looked like altered versions of others he'd seen in the territorial records.

"You're early," Carmen said as he approached.

"So are you. And you look like you didn't sleep much."

89

She managed a tired smile. "I spent most of the night going through shipping records at the telegraph office. What I found..." She shook her head. "It's worse than we thought."

From her bag, she produced a manila envelope thick with papers. "Union Pacific shipping manifests for the past eighteen months. Cross-referenced with the brand registrations you found yesterday and the dates of your various assignments."

Cord opened the envelope and found himself looking at meticulous documentation that made his stomach turn. Column after column of figures showed cattle shipments leaving Cheyenne under Blackwood's name, but the timing told the real story.

"The Heinrich herd," he said, running his finger down a manifest dated three weeks after Heinrich's arrest. "Four hundred head shipped to Chicago under Blackwood's consignment. But Heinrich only owned about two hundred cattle."

"Look at the manifest two lines down," Carmen said.

Cord's eyes found the entry: "Recovered stolen cattle - various small brands - consigned to S. Blackwood, Denver." The shipping date was four days after Heinrich's cattle had supposedly been returned to their rightful owners.

"I delivered these cattle to a man claiming to represent the Territorial Livestock Association," Cord said slowly. "He had papers, official documentation..."

"Forged, most likely. Or signed by someone in Blackwood's employ." Carmen pointed to another manifest. "Here's the Mitchell herd. And here's the Yoshida horses you recovered last month. All of it shipped east under Blackwood's name within days of being 'returned' to their owners."

The pattern was inescapable. Every animal Cord had recovered in his role as territorial marshal had ended up in Blackwood's operation, rebranded and shipped to market as legitimate stock. The families he'd thought he was helping had never seen their animals again.

"How many head are we talking about?" he asked.

Carmen had clearly done the mathematics. "Based on shipping records alone? Nearly three thousand cattle, four hundred horses, and roughly two hundred sheep over the past fourteen months. Conservative market value of about sixty thousand dollars."

Sixty thousand dollars. More money than most territorial ranchers would see in a lifetime, stolen through a system that used the law itself as a weapon.

"The railroad officials must know," Cord said. "They're handling the shipping, processing the manifests, collecting the fees."

"More than know. They're partners." Carmen produced another document from her envelope. "This is a copy of an exclusive shipping contract between the Union Pacific and Blackwood Cattle Company. Guaranteed rail cars, reduced shipping rates, priority loading - all in exchange for a minimum of five thousand head per year."

Cord studied the contract. The terms were extraordinarily favorable, the kind of deal the railroad would only offer to ensure a massive, steady flow of business. But five thousand head was far more than Blackwood's legitimate operation could provide, which meant...

"The stolen cattle aren't just a side business," he realized. "They're essential to meeting his shipping commitments."

"Exactly. Without the animals you've been recovering, Blackwood couldn't fulfill his contract with the railroad. And without that contract, he couldn't offer the kind of volume and reliability that's made him one of the territory's most powerful cattle barons."

"Who signed this for the railroad?"

Carmen pointed to a signature at the bottom of the document. "Marcus Dalton, Regional Freight Manager. He's been with Union Pacific for eight years, worked his way up from yard supervisor to his current position. He also happens to own a rather expensive house in Denver and sends his children to private schools back east."

"On a railroad manager's salary?"

"That would be difficult, yes."

The implications were staggering. The Union Pacific wasn't just a customer in this scheme - they were active participants, using their monopoly on transportation to ensure Blackwood's operation remained profitable. Every stolen cow, every appropriated horse, every family destroyed through legal manipulation ultimately served the railroad's need for guaranteed cargo.

"There's more," Carmen said. "The contract requires Union Pacific to provide certain... services... beyond simple transportation."

She handed him another document, this one showing payment authorizations. "Security services, cargo inspection, documentation processing. All handled by railroad personnel, all paid for by Blackwood."

"What kind of security services?"

"The kind that make sure inconvenient questions don't get asked about brands or ownership documents." Carmen's voice carried an edge of anger. "Deputy Marshal Frank Rawlings has been on Blackwood's payroll for over a year. Officially, he provides federal oversight of interstate cattle shipments. Unofficially..."

"He makes sure stolen cattle look legitimate on federal shipping documents."

"And ensures that any complaints about missing livestock get lost in bureaucratic channels." Carmen pulled out a telegram transcript. "This is from last month. Rawlings to Dalton: 'Heinrich family inquiry contained. No federal investigation warranted. Proceed with scheduled shipments.'"

Cord remembered Heinrich's desperate attempts to contact federal authorities, his insistence that territorial officials were corrupt. The man had been right, but his appeals for help had been intercepted by the very federal officer who should have protected him.

"How deep does this go?" Cord asked.

"I'm not sure yet. But I know it extends beyond Wyoming Territory. Some of these shipments are going to stockyards in Colorado and Nebraska before heading east. That suggests coordination across territorial boundaries."

The scope of the operation was becoming clear. This wasn't just territorial corruption - it was an interstate conspiracy involving railroad executives, federal marshals, and territorial officials. A network designed to systematically loot the resources of small ranchers and homesteaders for the benefit of large corporate interests.

"We need to see the actual shipping operation," Cord said. "Watch how they handle the cattle, see who's involved in the loading and documentation."

Carmen glanced toward the main office building. "The next major shipment goes out tomorrow morning. Five cars, mixed cattle, all consigned to Blackwood. If we could observe the loading process..."

"Too dangerous in daylight with this many people around. But tonight, after the yard workers go home..." Cord folded the documents and handed them back to her. "Can you get us access to the shipping office? I want to see the original manifests, not just the copies."

"I think so. There's a night telegraph operator who... owes me a favor."

The way she said it made Cord wonder again about her true background. Telegraph operators didn't usually have the kind of knowledge she'd displayed, or the access to sensitive railroad documents. But those questions could wait. Right now, they needed evidence solid enough to challenge a conspiracy that reached from territorial courts to federal agencies.

"Meet me behind the grain elevator at ten o'clock tonight," he said. "And Carmen? Bring a camera if you can find one. We're going to need photographic proof of what we discover."

"You think they'll try to deny the documents?"

"I think when we expose this, they're going to claim everything is forged. We need evidence they can't dispute."

As they prepared to leave separately, Cord caught sight of a familiar figure near the loading chutes. Deputy Marshal Frank Rawlings stood talking with a well-dressed man in a railroad supervisor's uniform - Marcus Dalton, presumably. Even at a distance, their conversation looked intense, urgent.

"They're worried about something," Carmen observed, following his gaze.

"Probably my sudden interest in brand registrations and shipping records. Hayes might have warned them that I'm asking inconvenient questions."

Rawlings gestured toward the cattle pens, and Dalton nodded, making notes in a leather portfolio. They were clearly coordinating something, making sure their next shipment went smoothly despite whatever complications Cord might represent.

"We need to be careful tonight," Carmen said. "If they suspect we're getting close to the truth..."

"I know." Cord watched the two men shake hands and part ways, Rawlings heading toward the telegraph office, Dalton returning to the railroad building. "But we're past the point of being careful. Too many families have been destroyed for us to worry about our own safety now."

Carmen nodded, but he could see the worry in her eyes. She understood better than most what happened to people who challenged powerful interests in territorial Wyoming. Her own family's fate proved that legal channels offered no protection against well-connected criminals.

"Ten o'clock," she said.

"Ten o'clock."

As Cord walked back toward town, he thought about the shipping manifests, the exclusive contracts, the systematic theft masquerading as law enforcement. Three thousand head of cattle, four hundred horses, sixty thousand dollars in stolen livestock. And behind it all, a network of corruption that stretched from territorial officials to railroad executives to federal marshals.

But they had something the conspirators didn't expect: detailed documentation of their crimes, and two people willing to risk everything to expose the truth.

Tonight, they would gather the final pieces of evidence. Tomorrow, they would decide how to use it.

The only question was whether they would live long enough to see justice done.

Chapter 11: Carmen's Secret

The abandoned line shack sat in a grove of cottonwoods three miles south of Cheyenne, its weathered boards gray as old bones in the moonlight. Cord had suggested the meeting place after their discovery of the railroad connection—too many ears in town now, too many people watching. Carmen had agreed without hesitation, which told him she understood the danger they were both in.

She was already waiting when he arrived, her horse tethered in the shadows behind the shack. Through the single window, he could see the warm glow of a small lantern. The scene felt oddly domestic, as if they were meeting for some clandestine romance rather than to plan the downfall of a territorial conspiracy.

Which, Cord reflected as he dismounted, wasn't entirely inaccurate. Over the past three days of working together, something had shifted between them. The shared danger, the careful trust they'd built, the way she'd looked at him when they discovered Dalton's shipping contracts—it had all combined into something that went beyond their mutual interest in exposing Blackwood.

"You're late," she said as he pushed through the door.

"Had to make sure I wasn't followed. Hayes has men watching the hotel." Cord settled onto a wooden crate across from where she sat on an old blanket. "After what we found today, I don't think we can assume we're safe anywhere in town."

The lantern cast dancing shadows on her face, highlighting the worry lines around her eyes. She looked tired, he realized. Not just from the day's work, but from something deeper—a weariness that came from carrying secrets too long.

"There's something I need to tell you," she said. "Something I should have told you before we got in this deep."

Cord had been expecting this. Her knowledge of the operation, her access to information, the way she'd known exactly where to look for evidence—it all suggested she had motives beyond simple civic duty.

"Go ahead."

Carmen took a breath, her hands folded in her lap. "My real name isn't Carmen Torres. It's Carmen Alejandra de Vega y Santos."

The names carried weight—old Spanish nobility, the kind that came with land grants dating back to Mexican rule. Cord kept his expression neutral, waiting.

"My family owned the Rancho de los Santos Hermanos," she continued. "Fifty thousand acres in the valley south of here, granted to my great-grandfather by the Mexican government in 1821. We ran cattle, raised horses. It was... it was a good life."

"Was?"

"Silas Blackwood wanted our land. The railroad was coming through, and our ranch controlled the best route to the southern cattle ranges. He made offers. We refused." Her voice hardened. "So he found other ways."

Cord leaned forward. "What kind of ways?"

"Legal manipulations. The Treaty of Guadalupe Hidalgo guaranteed that Mexican land grants would be honored by the American government, but proving ownership required navigating American courts with American law. Blackwood's attorneys challenged our grant, claimed the boundary markers had been moved, questioned the validity of the original documents."

"And?"

"And we discovered that territorial officials had been... influenced. Land commissioners who should have been impartial suddenly found our paperwork incomplete. Survey records went missing. Witnesses to boundary agreements developed convenient memory problems." Carmen's hands clenched into fists. "It took three years, but Blackwood eventually got what he wanted. The territorial court ruled that our grant was invalid due to insufficient documentation."

Cord thought of the shipping records they'd found, the careful coordination between railroad officials and territorial authorities. "When was this?"

"Two years ago. My father... he didn't survive seeing his family's legacy stolen through legal trickery. He died six months after we lost the ranch." Her voice caught slightly.

"My mother and younger brother moved to California. I stayed."

"Why?"

Carmen looked up at him, and in her dark eyes he saw something he recognized—the same cold determination he felt when tracking dangerous men.

"Because someone had to make sure Blackwood paid for what he did. And because I realized we weren't the only family he'd destroyed."

Now Cord understood. "That's why you took the job at the telegraph office."

"I needed to see the communications between Blackwood's people and the territorial officials. I needed to understand how the operation worked." She stood and began pacing in the small space. "What I discovered was worse than I imagined. It wasn't just our ranch—it was systematic. Mexican families, small homesteaders, anyone who stood in the way of Blackwood's expansion."

"Including the ranchers I went after."

"You were just the most recent tool. Before you, there were other marshals, territorial officials, even some Army officers who could be convinced that certain operations were threats to territorial security." Carmen stopped pacing and looked at him. "You're very good at what you do, Cord. That made you particularly valuable."

The compliment stung rather than pleased him. "Valuable enough to lie to for three days?"

"I didn't lie to you. I just... didn't tell you everything."

"What else haven't you told me?"

Carmen reached into her jacket and pulled out a leather portfolio. "I've been gathering evidence for two years. Not just on your cases—on all of it. The legal manipulations, the bribed officials, the falsified documents." She handed him the portfolio. "Three other Mexican families have lost their grants the same way we did. Twelve small ranching operations have been destroyed through legal challenges that shouldn't have succeeded. And now, with your help, I know about the cattle theft and brand manipulation."

Cord opened the portfolio and found himself looking at the most comprehensive documentation of corruption he'd ever seen. Court records, land deeds, telegraph copies, shipping manifests, even photographs of altered boundary markers and suspicious brand work.

"This is..." He looked up at her. "This is enough to bring down half the territorial government."

"That's the idea."

"Why didn't you take this to federal authorities two years ago?"

Carmen's laugh was bitter. "Who? Deputy Marshal Rawlings, who's been taking Blackwood's money? Territorial Commissioner Walsh, whose signature appears on every fraudulent land transfer? Judge Hamilton, who somehow always rules in favor of Blackwood's legal challenges?"

Cord understood. The corruption wasn't just deep—it was comprehensive. Every institution that should have protected people like Carmen's family had been compromised.

"So you decided to handle it yourself."

"I decided to gather enough evidence that even corrupt officials couldn't ignore it. Evidence so overwhelming that someone, somewhere in the federal government would have to act." She sat back down across from him. "But I needed help. I needed someone with the skills to uncover the operational details, someone who understood how the theft and fraud actually worked."

"Someone like me."

"Someone exactly like you."

They sat in silence for a moment, the lantern flickering between them. Outside, night birds called through the cottonwoods, and somewhere in the distance a coyote howled. Normal sounds of the territory, unchanged by the human scheming that had destroyed so many lives.

"There's more," Carmen said quietly. "Other families affected by this. People who don't have the resources or knowledge to fight back. Mexican ranchers south of the border who've had cattle stolen and shipped through Blackwood's operation. Lakota families whose treaty rights have been violated for the sake of Blackwood's expansion."

Cord thought of Thomas Running Bear's words about stolen horses and violated boundaries. "How widespread is this?"

"I think we've only seen the beginning. Blackwood isn't just building a cattle empire—he's systematically eliminating anyone who might challenge his control of territorial resources." Carmen leaned forward, her voice intense. "The evidence we've gathered over the past few days, combined with what I've collected over two years... we could expose the entire network."

"And get ourselves killed in the process."

"Probably." She met his gaze steadily. "But what's the alternative? Let him continue destroying families? Let him turn the entire territory into his personal kingdom?"

Cord closed the portfolio and set it aside. Here was the question that had been building for days: what was he willing to risk to make this right?

"There's something else," Carmen said, and her voice had changed, become softer. "Something personal."

"What?"

"These past few days, working with you... it's not what I expected when I decided to manipulate you into helping me."

The admission hung between them like smoke from the lantern. Cord had felt it too—the way their partnership had evolved from mutual necessity into something deeper. The moments when their hands had touched while examining documents. The way she'd looked at him when they discovered the full extent of the railroad conspiracy. The careful distance she maintained, as if afraid of getting too close.

"What did you expect?"

"I expected to use your skills and your reputation to gather evidence. I expected you to be... a tool, like you were for Blackwood." She looked down at her hands. "I didn't expect to care what happened to you."

"Carmen..."

"I know it's impossible," she said quickly. "I'm a Mexican woman whose family has been destroyed by the system you represented. You're an Anglo lawman who spent over a year unknowingly helping that destruction. Even if we survive this, even if we somehow bring Blackwood down... there's no future for us."

But as she said it, she was looking at him with an expression that suggested she wished it could be otherwise. And Cord found himself wishing the same thing.

"Maybe," he said carefully, "we should worry about surviving this first. The future... we can figure that out later."

"You think there might be a later?"

Cord thought about the evidence they'd gathered, the network of corruption they were challenging, the powerful men who would kill to protect their interests. Then he thought about Carmen's determination, his own skills, and the righteous anger that had been building in him since the night Hayes revealed the truth.

"I think," he said, "that Silas Blackwood has gotten used to using other people's tools to do his dirty work. He's about to discover what happens when those tools get turned against him."

Carmen smiled—the first genuine smile he'd seen from her. "So we do this?"

"We do this."

She reached across the space between them and took his hand. Her fingers were warm, calloused from hard work, steady despite the danger they faced. "Whatever happens, Cord, I want you to know... working with you these past few days, it's reminded me why I believed in justice in the first place."

"Even though I helped destroy your family?"

"You didn't know. And when you found out the truth, you chose to do something about it." She squeezed his hand. "That's the kind of man I hoped you might be."

They sat there in the lamplight, holding hands like lovers while planning the downfall of a territorial conspiracy. Outside, the night sounds continued, peaceful and eternal. Inside, two people who should have been enemies prepared to risk everything for justice.

Tomorrow, they would begin the dangerous work of exposing Silas Blackwood and his network. Tonight, they had found something neither had expected—trust, partnership, and the beginning of something that might have been love under different circumstances.

"We should get back," Carmen said eventually. "Separately, different routes."

"I know." But neither of them moved to leave.

"This won't end well," she said. "Even if we succeed, even if we bring them all down... men like Blackwood don't forgive, and they don't forget."

"Then we'd better make sure we do this right the first time."

Carmen stood, and Cord rose with her. For a moment they faced each other in the small space, close enough that he could see the gold flecks in her dark eyes, smell the faint scent of sage in her hair.

"Cord..."

He leaned down and kissed her, gently, carefully, as if she might disappear at any moment. She kissed him back, her hand coming up to rest against his chest, over his heart.

When they broke apart, she rested her forehead against his. "This is foolish."

"Probably."

"We have work to do."

"We do."

But they stood there a moment longer, holding onto something that might be their only chance at this kind of connection. Then Carmen stepped back, picked up the lantern, and became once again the careful, determined woman who had spent two years planning her revenge against the system that destroyed her family.

"Three days," she said. "That's how long before the next big cattle shipment goes out on the Union Pacific. If we're going to expose this, that's our best chance."

"Then we'd better get busy."

They left separately, as planned. Cord rode back toward Cheyenne through the darkness, thinking about evidence and conspiracies and the dangerous game they were about to play. But mostly he thought about the woman who had trusted him with her secrets, her mission, and for one brief moment, her heart.

Three days to bring down an empire. It would have to be enough.

Chapter 12: The Lakota Angle

The morning mist clung to the Laramie River as Cord made his way to the agreed meeting place, a grove of willows two miles upstream from town. Thomas Running Bear had sent word through a half-breed trader that he needed to speak with the marshal about stolen horses and broken promises. Given everything Cord had learned about Blackwood's operation, he suspected this conversation would add another layer to an already complex conspiracy.

Running Bear was waiting in the shadows of the largest willow, his presence so still and natural he seemed part of the landscape itself. He wore a mixture of traditional and white man's clothing—buckskin leggings under a wool shirt, his long black hair braided with eagle feathers. His weathered face bore the kind of lines that came from squinting into prairie wind and making difficult decisions for his people.

"Marshal," he said, stepping forward as Cord approached.

"Thomas." Cord had known Running Bear for three years, ever since a dispute over water rights had brought them together. Unlike many reservation Indians who'd been broken by government policies, Running Bear maintained the dignity and bearing of a man who remembered when his people had been free. "You said you had information about stolen livestock."

"More than that." Running Bear gestured toward a fallen log, inviting Cord to sit. "I have proof of things that should concern any man who believes in justice."

From a leather pouch, Running Bear produced a collection of documents—some official papers, others handwritten notes, and several crude maps drawn on what looked like pages torn from account books.

"For two seasons, cattle and horses have disappeared from Lakota herds," Running Bear began. "Not the random theft you might expect from desperate men, but organized raids that take specific animals and leave others untouched."

Cord examined the first document, a Bureau of Indian Affairs report listing livestock losses on the Pine Ridge Reservation. The numbers were staggering—over eight hundred head of cattle and two hundred horses reported stolen in the past eighteen months.

"The Indian Agent tells us these are probably raids by hostile bands," Running Bear continued, "but we know better. Hostile Lakota would take horses for war and meat for survival. They would not steal cattle branded for the white man's market."

"What makes you think otherwise?"

Running Bear unfolded one of his hand-drawn maps. "My nephew works as a scout for the Army. Last month, he followed fresh cattle tracks from our land toward Cheyenne. Fifty head, driven by experienced cowboys, not warriors. The trail led to a holding pen fifteen miles south of the city."

Cord studied the map, noting the location Running Bear had marked. It was uncomfortably close to one of the areas where he'd "recovered" stolen cattle for return to their rightful owners.

"There's more," Running Bear said, producing a photograph. "This was taken by a newspaperman from back east, someone writing about reservation life. He didn't understand what he was seeing, but I did."

The photograph showed a corral full of cattle bearing what appeared to be Lakota brands—simple geometric designs that differed from the more complex marks used by white ranchers. But something about the brands looked wrong, as if they'd been recently altered.

"These are our cattle," Running Bear said, pointing to specific animals in the photograph. "But see here, and here?" He indicated several brands that looked like they'd been modified with additional lines and marks. "Someone has changed our brands to make them look like white ranchers' marks."

Cord felt the familiar cold sensation of another piece falling into place. "Where was this photograph taken?"

"At the Blackwood shipping facility outside Denver. The newspaperman was doing a story about large-scale ranching operations." Running Bear's voice carried bitter irony. "He thought he was documenting American business success."

The implications were staggering. Not only was Blackwood stealing from small white ranchers through legal manipulation, he was conducting organized raids on reservation herds and altering the brands to make the theft appear legitimate. The scale of the operation was far beyond what Cord had imagined.

"The federal government has to know," Cord said. "These are treaty violations. Theft from reservation land falls under federal jurisdiction."

Running Bear's expression was grim. "That's what we thought. We sent delegations to the Indian Agent, to the territorial governor, even to Washington. We provided evidence, witness statements, maps showing where the cattle had been taken."

"And?"

"And we were told that the federal government takes Indian complaints very seriously, but that investigations take time. Meanwhile, the theft continued." Running Bear pulled out another document. "This is a letter from the Bureau of Indian Affairs to Agent Morrison at Pine Ridge, dated last month."

Cord read the letter, his jaw tightening with each line. The Bureau acknowledged the livestock losses but suggested they were probably the result of "poor record-keeping by tribal members unfamiliar with proper accounting methods." The letter recommended "more careful inventory procedures" rather than investigation of theft.

"They're dismissing your complaints as incompetence," Cord said.

"While the real thieves continue their work with government protection." Running Bear produced the most damaging document yet—a telegram transcript dated just two weeks earlier. "My nephew has friends among the Army telegraphers. This message went from Agent Morrison to Deputy Marshal Rawlings."

Cord read the telegram:

RAWLINGS CHEYENNE STOP LAKOTA DELEGATION REQUESTING FEDERAL INVESTIGATION STOP RECOMMEND NO ACTION STOP TRIBAL COMPLAINTS LACK CREDIBILITY STOP NORMAL BUSINESS OPERATIONS SHOULD CONTINUE STOP MORRISON

The web of corruption was more extensive than Cord had realized. Not only were territorial and railroad officials involved, but federal Indian agents were actively suppressing evidence of the theft. The system wasn't just broken—it was deliberately designed to enable this kind of exploitation.

"There's something else," Running Bear said. "Something that connects to your recent activities."

He handed Cord a list of names—Lakota families who had lost cattle in recent months. Next to several names were notes indicating when and where the animals had been stolen.

"The Stands Alone family lost forty head three months ago," Running Bear said, pointing to one entry. "The theft occurred the same week you arrested a white rancher named Ferguson for rustling."

Cord remembered the Ferguson case. He'd tracked stolen cattle to the man's ranch and arrested him despite Ferguson's insistence that he'd bought the animals legitimately. The cattle had been "returned" to their rightful owner—or so Cord had thought.

"You think Ferguson was buying stolen Lakota cattle?"

"I think Ferguson was a convenient scapegoat when someone needed to cover their tracks." Running Bear's voice was patient but firm. "The same week our cattle disappeared, your man Ferguson gets arrested for rustling. The stolen animals get 'recovered' and returned to their 'rightful owner'—who happens to be connected to Blackwood's operation."

The pattern was becoming sickeningly clear. When Blackwood's people needed to cover major thefts from the reservation, they would arrange for some small-time rancher to be caught with obviously stolen cattle. Cord would arrest the scapegoat, "recover" the stolen animals, and deliver them to someone claiming to represent their legitimate owner. The Lakota would be told their complaints were being investigated, while their cattle ended up in Blackwood's shipping network.

"How many families have lost livestock this way?" Cord asked.

"Thirty-seven Lakota families in the past eighteen months. But it's not just our people." Running Bear leaned forward.

"The Crow reservation to the north has reported similar losses. The Northern Cheyenne as well. All dismissed by Indian agents as poor record-keeping or internal disputes."

"A coordinated campaign."

"Targeting people the government considers expendable." Running Bear's words carried the weight of bitter experience. "Indian cattle, Mexican land grants, small homesteads—anyone without political connections becomes fair game."

Cord thought about Carmen's family, about the Heinrich and Mitchell ranches, about the systematic destruction of anyone who stood in the way of large corporate interests. The common thread wasn't just Blackwood's greed—it was the government's willingness to sacrifice the powerless for the benefit of the connected.

"Why come to me now?" he asked. "Why not take this to federal authorities in Denver or Washington?"

Running Bear was quiet for a long moment, studying Cord's face. "Because my nephew tells me you've been asking questions lately. Questions about brand registrations and shipping records. Questions that make certain people nervous."

"You've been watching me."

"We watch everyone who might affect our people's welfare. But lately, we think maybe you've learned what we learned long ago—that the law serves those who can afford to buy it."

It was a harsh assessment, but Cord couldn't argue with it. His recent discoveries had shown him exactly how the legal system could be perverted to serve criminal purposes.

"What do you want from me?"

"Justice," Running Bear said simply. "Our people have tried working within the white man's system. We've followed every proper procedure, filed every required complaint, provided every piece of evidence the government requested. And our cattle are still being stolen."

"So you want me to do what? Arrest Blackwood? Rawlings? Morrison?"

"I want you to remember that justice isn't about whose law gets enforced—it's about right and wrong." Running Bear stood, gathering his documents. "You have skills, Marshal. You have a reputation. People listen when you speak."

"Some people. Not the ones who matter."

"Maybe. But if a respected territorial marshal started asking the right questions, started demanding answers from federal officials, started treating Indian complaints as seriously as white complaints..." Running Bear shrugged. "It might be harder for them to dismiss us as ignorant savages who can't count our own cattle."

Cord stood as well, his mind racing through the implications of what he'd learned. The corruption wasn't just about cattle theft or land fraud—it was about a systematic policy of dispossessing anyone who lacked political power. Indians, Mexicans, small farmers, anyone who stood in the way of corporate expansion.

"There's something else you should know," Running Bear said as they prepared to part. "Word has come down from the reservation that federal marshals are planning a major operation next week. Something about arresting rustlers and recovering stolen cattle."

"What kind of operation?"

"The kind where a lot of small ranchers and homesteaders get arrested, and a lot of cattle get 'recovered' for their rightful owners." Running Bear's expression was grim. "My nephew heard Deputy Marshal Rawlings tell the Army commander that this operation would 'clean up' the territory's rustling problem once and for all."

The implication was clear. Blackwood and his associates were planning a massive roundup that would eliminate the last independent operators in the territory, using federal authority to accomplish what individual arrests hadn't achieved. And Cord would probably be expected to participate, using his reputation to legitimize the operation.

"How much time do we have?"

"A few days at most. The operation is planned to coincide with the next major cattle shipment east."

Cord nodded, understanding the timing. Clean out the competition, seize their assets, and ship everything east before anyone could challenge the legality of the arrests.

"Thomas," he said as Running Bear prepared to leave, "if I decide to act on this information, it's going to put your people at risk. Blackwood's operation has powerful protection."

"My people are already at risk," Running Bear replied. "We're being robbed systematically while the government claims to protect us. At least if you act, we'll know someone is willing to stand up for justice instead of just profit."

They parted without shaking hands—too dangerous if anyone was watching—but with an understanding that had been absent from their previous encounters. Cord was no longer just another government official to be cautiously managed. He was a potential ally in a fight against systematic corruption.

As Cord rode back toward Cheyenne, he thought about treaty violations and federal complicity, about Indian agents who suppressed evidence and deputy marshals who enabled theft. The corruption reached far beyond territorial officials and railroad executives. It extended to the highest levels of federal authority, involving people who were supposed to protect the powerless rather than exploit them.

But he also thought about Running Bear's challenge: justice isn't about whose law gets enforced—it's about right and wrong.

For over a year, Cord had enforced the law as it was written and administered. Now he was beginning to understand that sometimes, being lawful and being just were two very different things.

The question was whether he had the courage to choose justice over law, knowing it would cost him everything he'd built as a territorial marshal.

That answer, he realized, would come soon enough.

Chapter 13: Caught Between Worlds

Hayes was waiting in Cord's hotel room when he returned from his meeting with Thomas Running Bear, sitting in the single chair like he owned the place. The door had been locked, but locks had never been much of an obstacle for a man in Hayes's line of work. What troubled Cord more was the casual confidence of the intrusion—Hayes no longer bothered to maintain even the pretense of legality.

"Marshal," Hayes said, not bothering to stand. "Hear you've been having some interesting conversations lately."

Cord hung his hat on the bedpost and faced his supposed supervisor. In the afternoon light filtering through the dusty window, Hayes looked older and more dangerous than he had a week ago. The genial mask had slipped, revealing something predatory underneath.

"Nothing that concerns you," Cord said.

"Oh, but it does concern me. It concerns me greatly." Hayes pulled a folded paper from his jacket. "I have a warrant here for one Gustav Hoffman. Seems the old German has been rustling cattle again."

The paper looked official enough—territorial seal, proper signatures, all the legal formalities that made theft look like justice. Cord didn't need to examine it closely to know it was probably legitimate, signed by officials who were either corrupt or deceived.

"What's Hoffman supposed to have stolen this time?"

"Forty head of prime beef cattle belonging to the Territorial Grazing Association. Brands altered, ownership documents forged, the whole criminal enterprise." Hayes's voice carried mock sympathy. "Poor old man must have thought he could get away with it because he had friends in the marshal's office."

The accusation was so brazen it took Cord's breath away. Hoffman had been one of the most honest men he'd ever met, a German immigrant who'd built his small ranch through backbreaking work and careful husbandry. The idea that he would steal cattle was absurd—but absurdity had never stopped Hayes before.

"When did this alleged theft occur?"

"Last Tuesday. Same day you were asking questions at the territorial records office, as it happens." Hayes's smile was cold. "Interesting coincidence, don't you think?"

The timing made the trap obvious. Hoffman was being framed because Cord had started investigating, a message that any further curiosity would cost innocent people their freedom.

"Who reported the theft?"

"Anonymous tip. But we've got witnesses, evidence, even some of the stolen cattle recovered on Hoffman's property." Hayes stood, moving to the window. "Open and shut case, really. Should be simple enough for a marshal of your... experience."

"And if I refuse?"

Hayes turned from the window, his expression hardening. "Now why would you refuse to arrest a cattle thief? Unless, of course, you're starting to believe that enforcing territorial law is somehow... optional."

The threat hung between them like smoke from a poorly ventilated stove. Hayes was making it clear that Cord's cooperation was no longer a matter of employment—it was a matter of survival.

"I've seen Hoffman's operation," Cord said. "He barely has enough cattle to make a living. Where would he hide forty stolen head?"

"Amazing what desperate men can accomplish when they think they won't get caught." Hayes pulled out a pocket watch, checking the time. "The warrant needs to be served today, Marshal. Federal authorities are coordinating a territory-wide operation to clean up the rustling problem, and Hoffman is just the beginning."

There it was—the federal roundup Running Bear had warned him about. A coordinated campaign to arrest every small rancher and homesteader who might pose a threat to Blackwood's expansion plans. And they expected Cord to legitimize it with his reputation for honest law enforcement.

"What if I find evidence that Hoffman's innocent?"

Hayes's laugh was genuinely amused. "Evidence? Marshal, you're not a judge or a jury. You're a law enforcement officer. Your job is to serve the warrant and bring in the suspect. What happens after that is up to the territorial courts."

"The same courts that decided the Heinrich and Mitchell cases?"

The humor faded from Hayes's expression. "I'd be very careful about questioning judicial integrity, Marshal. That kind of talk could be seen as seditious, especially coming from a federal officer."

"I'm a territorial marshal, not a federal officer."

"Are you?" Hayes reached into his jacket and produced another document. "Because according to this commission, signed yesterday by Deputy Marshal Frank Rawlings, you're now operating under federal authority. Congratulations on the promotion."

Cord took the document, recognizing Rawlings's signature from the railroad documents he and Carmen had discovered. The commission was legitimate enough, giving him expanded authority to pursue cattle thieves across territorial boundaries. It also placed him directly under federal oversight, eliminating any possibility of independent action.

"You've been planning this for a while," Cord said.

"We've been planning this since the day you proved you could track a stolen horse through a blizzard," Hayes replied. "A man with your skills, working under proper supervision, could accomplish remarkable things."

"Such as?"

"Such as ensuring that the territory's resources are developed by people capable of using them efficiently. Such as making sure that federal treaty obligations are met without interference from... unqualified parties." Hayes moved closer, his voice dropping to a more intimate register. "Such as building a future where law enforcement serves progress instead of standing in its way."

The vision Hayes painted was seductive in its simplicity: order imposed by competent authority, resources allocated to those who could use them most effectively, progress unimpeded by the sentimental attachment of small operators to unprofitable land. It was the same argument powerful men had used throughout history to justify taking from the weak.

"And if I don't want to be part of that future?"

Hayes's smile returned, but it was cold as winter wind. "Then you'll discover that the territory can be a very dangerous place for someone without proper protection. Accidents happen, Marshal. Men disappear. Sometimes they're found weeks later, victims of hostile Indians or desperate outlaws."

The threat was unmistakable. Cooperate or die, with enough plausible deniability to avoid inconvenient questions.

Cord looked at the warrant in his hands, thinking about Gustav Hoffman's weathered face, his pride in the small ranch he'd built through honest work. Then he thought about the Heinrich family, about James Mitchell's wife crying as her husband was taken away, about Thomas

Running Bear's patient dignity in the face of systematic theft.

"No," he said quietly.

"I'm sorry?"

"No. I won't arrest Gustav Hoffman for cattle theft because Gustav Hoffman isn't a cattle thief." Cord set the warrant on the bed. "And I won't be part of whatever federal operation you're planning."

Hayes stared at him for a long moment, as if he couldn't quite believe what he was hearing. "Marshal, I don't think you understand the situation."

"I understand it perfectly. You want me to arrest innocent people so Blackwood can steal their land and cattle. You want me to use my reputation to legitimize systematic theft and fraud." Cord moved closer to Hayes, his voice hardening. "What I don't understand is how you can look at yourself in the mirror."

"Careful, Marshal."

"No, I'm done being careful. I'm done pretending that what we've been doing is law enforcement instead of organized crime." Cord reached for his badge, unpinning it from his vest. "I'm done being Silas Blackwood's hired gun."

He tossed the badge onto the bed next to the warrant.

Hayes looked at the discarded badge, then back at Cord. "You're making a very serious mistake."

"The serious mistake was trusting you in the first place."

"Do you have any idea what you're giving up? The money, the position, the protection?" Hayes's voice carried genuine puzzlement, as if he couldn't comprehend anyone refusing such obvious benefits. "You could be wealthy, Marshal. Respected. Protected."

"By who? Men like Blackwood? Railroad executives? Federal officials who violate treaties and steal from reservations?" Cord shook his head. "That's not protection —it's complicity."

Hayes picked up the badge and warrant, slipping both into his jacket. "Very well. But understand this, Marshal—or should I say, former Marshal—you've just made yourself a problem. And Mr. Blackwood has very effective ways of solving problems."

"Let him try."

"Oh, he will. But it won't be quick, and it won't be clean." Hayes moved toward the door, pausing with his hand on the knob. "You have skills, I'll grant you that. But skills won't protect the people you care about. Miss Torres, for instance. Telegraph operators can have accidents too."

The threat against Carmen ignited something cold and deadly in Cord's chest. "If you touch her—"

"Then what? You'll track me down? Arrest me?" Hayes's laugh was mocking. "With what authority? Under whose law? You just threw away the only thing that made you dangerous."

Hayes opened the door, then turned back one final time. "You have until sunset to reconsider, Marshal. After that, you become just another obstacle to progress. And we both know what happens to obstacles."

The door closed behind him with a soft click, leaving Cord alone with the enormity of what he'd just done. In the space of five minutes, he'd thrown away his career, his income, his official protection, and quite possibly his life. But for the first time in over a year, he felt clean.

He moved to the window and watched Hayes emerge from the hotel, walking with the confident stride of a man who owned the territory. Across the street, two other men fell into step behind him—Blackwood's hired guns, probably, ready to implement whatever solution their employer favored for former employees who knew too much.

Cord began packing his few belongings, moving with the methodical efficiency of a man who'd spent years traveling light. He'd need to leave the hotel soon, find somewhere safe to plan his next moves. But first, he needed to warn Carmen.

A soft knock at the door made him freeze. If Hayes had decided not to wait until sunset...

"Cord? It's me."

Carmen's voice. He opened the door carefully, checking the hallway before letting her in.

"I saw Hayes leaving," she said, noting his packed saddlebags. "From your expression, I'd guess the conversation didn't go well."

"He wanted me to arrest Gustav Hoffman for rustling his own cattle. I refused."

Carmen's face went pale. "Oh, God. You broke with them completely?"

"Completely." Cord resumed packing. "Which means we're both in danger now. Hayes made it clear that you're a target too."

"I expected that." Carmen moved to the window, peering through the curtains. "There are men watching the hotel. Three that I can see, probably more I can't."

"We need to get out of Cheyenne. Tonight."

"Where will we go?"

Cord thought about Running Bear's evidence, about the systematic theft from reservations and small ranches, about the federal operation planned to eliminate the last independent operators in the territory. Then he thought about Gustav Hoffman, probably sitting on his porch right now, unaware that federal marshals were planning to arrest him for crimes he didn't commit.

"We're going to warn Hoffman," he said. "And then we're going to find every small rancher and homesteader who's about to be framed for cattle theft. We're going to tell them what's coming and help them prepare."

"That's not a plan—that's suicide. Blackwood has unlimited resources, federal protection, and men who kill for money."

"Maybe. But he's also gotten careless. He's used to using other people's authority to do his dirty work." Cord shouldered his rifle and saddlebags. "Now he'll have to come at us directly, without the cover of legal process. That changes the game considerably."

Carmen studied his face, seeing something that made her nod slowly. "You're not running from this."

"No. I'm done running from anything."

"Then we'd better be very smart about how we fight it." She moved away from the window. "I have contacts among the small ranchers, people whose families have been hurt by this operation. They've been waiting for someone to organize resistance."

"What kind of resistance?"

"The kind that uses evidence instead of guns, at least at first. But if Blackwood's men start shooting..." Carmen's expression hardened. "Well, farmers and ranchers know how to protect what's theirs."

Cord looked around the hotel room one final time, then blew out the lamp. Outside, sunset was painting the sky the color of blood, and somewhere in the darkness, men were planning his death.

But for the first time since he'd pinned on a badge, Cord Maddox felt like he was on the right side of a fight.

Now he just had to survive it.

Chapter 14: Going Underground

The abandoned mining cabin sat in a canyon fifteen miles northwest of Cheyenne, hidden among granite outcroppings and scrub pine where only someone who knew the territory intimately would think to look. Cord had discovered it three years earlier while tracking rustlers, noting its concealed location and fresh water source. Now it served as headquarters for what Gustav Hoffman had started calling "the resistance."

"Five more families confirmed," Carmen reported, consulting a list written on the back of an old envelope. "The Jensons, the O'Briens, the Martinez family, the Kowalskis, and old Pete Yamamoto. All received visits from federal marshals in the past week, all warned about pending investigations into cattle theft."

Cord looked up from the map spread across the cabin's rough wooden table. Red marks indicated ranches that had already been targeted, blue marks showed families who'd received warnings, and black marks represented operations that had been eliminated entirely. The pattern was unmistakable—Blackwood's network was systematically clearing the territory of small operators.

"How much time do they think we have?" asked Gustav Hoffman.

The German immigrant had aged visibly in the five days since Cord had warned him about the arrest warrant. The proud bearing was still there, but worry lines had deepened around his eyes. His small ranch represented twenty years of backbreaking work, and the thought of losing it to manufactured charges had shaken him more than he wanted to admit.

"Not long," Carmen said. "I intercepted a telegraph message yesterday from Deputy Marshal Rawlings to someone in Denver. The federal operation is scheduled to begin Monday morning—six days from now."

Six days. Cord studied the map, counting the families who would be swept up in the coordinated arrests. Thirty-seven small operations, representing hundreds of people who would lose everything they'd built.

"What about evidence?" asked Maria Santos, a young Mexican woman whose family had lost their sheep ranch to legal manipulation six months earlier. "We can prove these charges are false, can't we?"

"Some of them," Cord replied. "But proving innocence won't matter if the courts are corrupt. We need to expose the entire operation—show that it's systematic fraud, not individual crimes."

From his saddlebags, he pulled out the collection of documents they'd gathered over the past week. Working together, the group had compiled an impressive dossier: shipping records showing impossible cattle volumes, brand registrations that coincided suspiciously with arrests, financial records linking territorial officials to Blackwood's operation, even photographs of altered brands and forged documents.

"The problem," said Tom O'Brien, a weathered Irishman whose small ranch bordered the Union Pacific tracks, "is getting anyone in authority to look at this evidence. Every official we've tried to contact either ignores us or claims jurisdiction problems."

"That's because the corruption reaches every level of territorial authority," Carmen said. "Local sheriffs, territorial commissioners, federal marshals—they're all either bought or intimidated."

"So what do we do?" asked Elena Martinez, whose family had been struggling since her husband's arrest on trumped-up horse theft charges. "Hide in the mountains until they find us anyway?"

Cord had been wrestling with the same question. They had evidence of massive fraud and systematic corruption, but no legitimate authority willing to act on it. Traditional legal channels had been compromised, leaving them in the impossible position of knowing about crimes they couldn't prosecute.

"There might be another option," Carmen said carefully. "Something I heard about in a telegraph message two days ago."

The room fell silent. Carmen's intelligence from her position at the telegraph office had been invaluable, but the danger to her was increasing daily. Hayes's men were watching the office, and sooner or later they would connect her absences to the resistance activities.

"What kind of option?" Cord asked.

"A federal marshal from Denver is coming to investigate complaints about territorial law enforcement. Someone named Lucas Garrett—I've never seen his name in any of the corrupt communications."

Hoffman leaned forward. "A real federal marshal? Not another one of Blackwood's men?"

"That's what I'm hoping. The message came directly from the federal courthouse in Denver, not through territorial channels. And Deputy Marshal Rawlings seemed... upset about it."

Cord considered the implications. If Garrett was legitimate, he might represent their only chance to present evidence to uncorrupted federal authority. But if he was another plant, approaching him would expose the entire resistance network.

"When does he arrive?" he asked.

"Tomorrow afternoon, according to the message. He's supposed to meet with territorial officials and review recent law enforcement activities."

"Including my cases," Cord realized.

"Almost certainly. Which means he'll want to speak with you."

The irony wasn't lost on anyone in the room. For weeks, they'd been hiding from federal authority, and now their best hope might lie in approaching the very system they'd been evading.

"It's a trap," said O'Brien flatly. "Has to be. They know we're organizing resistance, so they send in someone who looks legitimate to draw us out."

"Maybe," Cord admitted. 'But what if it isn't? What if there are still honest federal marshals who don't know about the corruption?"

"Then we'd be fools not to try," said Maria Santos. "My family lost everything because we trusted the system to protect us. But maybe... maybe not everyone in the system is corrupt."

Cord looked around the cabin at the faces of people who'd lost homes, livelihoods, and family members to Blackwood's operation. They were farmers and ranchers, not professional revolutionaries. They wanted justice, not warfare.

"If we approach this Marshal Garrett," he said, "we'll need to be very careful. Assume Rawlings and his people will try to discredit anything we say."

"How?" asked Hoffman.

"Same way they always do. Paint us as criminals, claim our evidence is fabricated, suggest we're making false accusations to cover our own crimes." Cord traced patterns on the map with his finger. "Rawlings will probably tell Garrett that I went rogue, started working with rustlers, can't be trusted."

Carmen nodded. 'And they'll have documentation to support that story. Forged reports, planted evidence, witness statements from people who owe them favors."

"So we need more than just evidence," Elena Martinez said. "We need proof they can't discredit."

"Such as?"

"Witnesses they can't intimidate. Documentation they can't claim is forged. Evidence so overwhelming that even corrupt officials can't dismiss it."

Over the next several hours, they developed a plan that was either brilliant or suicidal, depending on one's perspective. They would approach Marshal Garrett, but not as fugitives seeking protection. Instead, they would present themselves as concerned citizens with evidence of systematic corruption—evidence so comprehensive and well-documented that even Rawlings couldn't discredit it.

"I'll return to the telegraph office tomorrow," Carmen said. "Try to intercept communications between Rawlings and his contacts. If Garrett is legitimate, Rawlings will be trying to control what information reaches him."

"Too dangerous," Cord objected. "Hayes knows you're involved with me."

"Which is why I need to maintain my cover as long as possible. If I disappear now, they'll know we're organized. If I keep working, I can provide intelligence about their countermoves."

It was a calculated risk, but Carmen was right. Her access to telegraph communications had been invaluable, and losing that capability now could be disastrous.

"What about the rest of us?" asked O'Brien.

"We document everything," Cord said. "Every family affected, every piece of stolen property, every corrupt official involved. We create a record so detailed that no honest investigator could ignore it."

"And if Garrett isn't honest?"

"Then we'll know we're on our own, and we'll act accordingly."

The meeting broke up near midnight, with each family representative carrying specific assignments. They would spread the word quietly, gather more evidence, and prepare for either salvation or final confrontation.

After the others left, Cord and Carmen stood outside the cabin, looking up at stars that seemed impossibly bright in the clear mountain air. The silence was peaceful, a stark contrast to the turmoil they faced.

"You know this probably won't work," Carmen said.

"Probably not. But it's better than hiding until they hunt us down one by one."

"And if Marshal Garrett turns out to be honest? What then?"

Cord considered the question. Even if they exposed Blackwood's operation, even if they brought down the network of corruption, the powerful interests behind it would remain. Corporate consolidation, government complicity, the systematic dispossession of small operators —those forces would continue under other names, through other methods.

"Then we'll have saved some families and maybe made things a little harder for the next Silas Blackwood," he said finally. "Sometimes that's the best you can do."

Carmen moved closer, and he put his arm around her shoulders. Despite everything—the danger, the uncertainty, the likelihood that they wouldn't survive the coming confrontation—he felt more at peace than he had in months.

"Whatever happens," she said quietly, "I'm glad we found each other."

"Even though I helped destroy your family's ranch?"

"You didn't know. And when you learned the truth, you chose to do something about it." She looked up at him. "That's what matters."

They stood there for a long time, two people who'd found love in the midst of conspiracy and corruption, holding onto each other while preparing to risk everything for justice.

Tomorrow would bring Marshal Garrett and the first test of whether the federal system contained any honest officials. If it did, they might have a chance. If it didn't...

Well, as Gustav Hoffman had said, they were already calling themselves "the resistance." Soon they might have to prove they deserved the name.

Chapter 15: The Marshal's Dilemma

Marshal Lucas Garrett was not what Cord had expected. The federal officer who stepped off the afternoon train from Denver looked more like a school teacher than a lawman—medium height, wire-rimmed spectacles, a careful way of moving that suggested thoughtfulness rather than physical prowess. But his handshake was firm, his gray eyes alert, and he carried himself with the quiet confidence of a man who'd learned to read situations quickly.

"Marshal Maddox," Garrett said as they met on the platform. "I've heard quite a lot about your work in this territory."

"I imagine you have," Cord replied carefully. "Though I suspect the stories vary depending on who's telling them."

Garrett's slight smile suggested he understood the implication. "Indeed they do. Which is why I prefer to form my own opinions based on direct observation and evidence."

They were being watched, Cord knew. Rawlings had positioned men throughout Cheyenne, and word of Garrett's arrival would already be spreading through the network of corrupt officials. Every word of this conversation would be reported within the hour.

"Deputy Marshal Rawlings sends his regrets," Garrett continued, consulting a pocket notebook. "He's apparently dealing with some urgent territorial business but hopes to brief me tomorrow morning."

"How convenient."

"Isn't it?" Garrett's tone remained neutral, but something in his expression suggested he was drawing his own conclusions about Rawlings's absence. "In the meantime, I was hoping you might help me understand some discrepancies I've noticed in recent law enforcement reports."

They walked toward the hotel, Garrett carrying a worn leather satchel that probably contained the federal records he'd been reviewing. Cord noted how the marshal's eyes constantly moved, cataloging faces, assessing potential threats, filing away details for later analysis. Whatever else Garrett might be, he wasn't naive about the dangers of his situation.

"What kind of discrepancies?" Cord asked.

"Unusual patterns in cattle theft arrests and recoveries. Complaints from territorial residents that don't match official reports. Questions about land transfers and brand registrations." Garrett paused. "And some very interesting communications between territorial officials and private interests."

The last comment was clearly a test, designed to gauge Cord's reaction and willingness to discuss sensitive topics. If Garrett was corrupt, admitting knowledge of such communications would be dangerous. If he was honest, remaining silent would be a missed opportunity.

"Such as communications between Deputy Marshal Rawlings and Silas Blackwood?" Cord asked.

Garrett stopped walking and turned to face him directly. For a moment, they stood in the middle of Cheyenne's main street, two federal officers taking each other's measure while the machinery of corruption churned around them.

"Among others," Garrett said finally. "Tell me, Marshal Maddox, in your professional opinion, how would you characterize the current state of law enforcement in Wyoming Territory?"

It was the moment of truth. Cord could give a careful, noncommittal answer that protected him from retaliation, or he could trust that Lucas Garrett represented what he appeared to be—an honest federal officer investigating corruption.

"Compromised," Cord said. "Systematically and deliberately compromised to serve private interests rather than public justice."

Garrett nodded slowly. "That's a serious allegation."

"It's a serious situation. Territorial marshals are being used to eliminate small ranchers through manufactured charges. Brand registrations are being manipulated to legitimize theft. Land grants are being challenged through corrupt legal processes. And federal officials are either participating or looking the other way."

"You have evidence to support these claims?"

"Extensive evidence. Documents, witness statements, financial records, shipping manifests—everything needed to prove systematic fraud."

"I'd like to see that evidence."

"And I'd like to know whether showing it to you would result in justice or simply alert the conspirators to destroy what proof remains."

They had reached the hotel, but neither man moved toward the entrance. Around them, Cheyenne's afternoon bustle continued, but Cord was intensely aware of the watchers in doorways and windows, the careful positioning of men who looked like drifters but moved with purpose.

"A reasonable concern," Garrett admitted. "Let me ask you this: if you were in my position, investigating allegations of territorial corruption while not knowing who could be trusted, how would you proceed?"

The question revealed more about Garrett's situation than hours of conversation might have. He was isolated, operating without reliable local contacts, trying to distinguish truth from deception in a web of competing interests and manufactured evidence.

"Carefully," Cord said. "And probably not by staying at the Palace Hotel, where every conversation gets reported to interested parties within the hour."

"You have a better suggestion?"

Cord made the decision that would either save or damn them all. "There's an abandoned mining cabin fifteen miles northwest of town. Canyon Creek Road, then follow the old mining trail to Bear Canyon. If you're there at sunset, you'll meet some people who can show you evidence that'll either make your career or get you killed."

Garrett wrote nothing down, but Cord could see him committing the directions to memory. "And if this is a trap?"

"Then you'll die having seen proof of the biggest territorial corruption case in federal history. If it isn't..." Cord shrugged. "You might actually be able to do something about it."

Before Garrett could respond, Deputy Marshal Frank Rawlings appeared around the corner, flanked by two men Cord recognized as Blackwood's hired guns. Rawlings wore his usual genial expression, but his eyes were hard as flint.

"Marshal Garrett!" Rawlings called out with forced heartiness. "Sorry I missed your arrival. Territorial business, you understand."

"Of course," Garrett replied smoothly. "I was just discussing recent law enforcement activities with Marshal Maddox."

"Was you?" Rawlings's smile never wavered, but his attention fixed on Cord with predatory intensity. "Hope he didn't fill your head with any wild stories. Poor Cord's been under a lot of strain lately—job pressures, you understand. Sometimes affects a man's judgment."

"I see. What kind of job pressures?"

"Oh, the usual. Difficult arrests, uncooperative suspects, that sort of thing." Rawlings moved closer, positioning himself between Garrett and Cord. "In fact, there's been some concern about Marshal Maddox's... reliability... in recent weeks."

"What kind of concern?"

Rawlings produced a folder from his jacket. "Reports of erratic behavior, unauthorized investigations, possible association with known criminals. Nothing proven, you understand, but troubling nonetheless."

Cord could guess what the folder contained—forged documents, manufactured witness statements, carefully constructed evidence designed to discredit anything he might tell Garrett. The same techniques used against the Heinrich family, against James Mitchell, against every small rancher who'd posed a threat to Blackwood's operation.

"Interesting," Garrett said, accepting the folder but not opening it. "I'll certainly review these materials carefully."

"I'm sure you will. In the meantime, might I suggest we continue this discussion somewhere more... private?" Rawlings gestured toward the hotel. "Territorial law enforcement is a complex subject, best discussed among professionals."

The invitation was clearly designed to isolate Garrett from Cord, to begin the process of shaping his understanding of the situation through carefully filtered information. If

Garrett accepted, Cord's chance to present evidence would be lost.

"Actually," Garrett said, "I'd prefer to conduct my own interviews and review before hearing official briefings. Professional habit, you understand."

Rawlings's smile tightened almost imperceptibly. "Of course. Though I should mention that Marshal Maddox is currently under investigation for several serious violations of federal law enforcement protocols."

"What kind of violations?"

"Failure to serve legitimate warrants, interference with federal operations, possible conspiracy with known criminals." Rawlings's tone remained conversational, but the implications were clear. "I'd hate for a distinguished federal marshal to be compromised by association with someone under such serious suspicion."

It was expertly done—a warning disguised as helpful advice, a threat wrapped in bureaucratic language. Associate with Cord, and find yourself targeted by the same machinery that destroyed territorial resistance.

"I appreciate the warning," Garrett said. "I'll certainly keep it in mind as I conduct my investigation."

"I'm sure you will. Deputy Morgan here will be happy to provide any assistance you might need." Rawlings indicated one of his companions, a lean man with the dead eyes of a professional killer. "He's very familiar with territorial law enforcement issues."

"How thoughtful."

After Rawlings and his men left, Garrett and Cord stood in uncomfortable silence for several moments. The federal marshal was clearly processing what he'd witnessed—the careful choreography of intimidation, the subtle threats, the systematic attempt to control information.

"Sunset," Garrett said finally.

"Sunset."

"If this is legitimate, Marshal Maddox, you're asking me to risk my career and possibly my life on the word of a man I met an hour ago."

"I'm asking you to risk those things for justice," Cord replied. "Which, unless I'm completely wrong about you, is what you swore an oath to uphold."

Garrett studied him for a long moment, then nodded. "Sunset it is."

As Cord walked away, he was acutely aware of the watchers in doorways, the careful positioning of Rawlings's men, the subtle net of surveillance that surrounded anyone who might threaten Blackwood's operation. By tomorrow, Rawlings would know about the planned meeting. By tomorrow night, the canyon might be full of hired guns instead of honest farmers seeking justice.

But for the first time since he'd thrown down his badge in Hayes's face, Cord felt genuinely hopeful. Lucas Garrett might be their salvation, or he might be another trap. Either way, they'd know by sunset.

At the telegraph office, Carmen was finishing her afternoon shift when Rawlings entered with two of his men. She'd been expecting something like this since Garrett's arrival, but her heart still jumped when she saw the cold calculation in the deputy marshal's eyes.

"Miss Torres," Rawlings said pleasantly. "I wonder if we might have a word?"

"Of course, Deputy Marshal. How can I help you?"

"I'm hoping you might be able to clarify some... irregularities... in recent telegraph traffic. Messages that seem to have been copied or delayed in transmission."

Carmen kept her expression neutral, though she knew her cover was blown. Someone had noticed the pattern of intercepted messages, probably connected it to the resistance activities, and drawn the obvious conclusions.

"I'm not sure what you mean," she said.

Rawlings smiled, but it didn't reach his eyes. "Of course you don't. Well, perhaps a more detailed discussion might refresh your memory. Somewhere private, where we won't be interrupted."

It wasn't a request, and Carmen knew it. She also knew that once Rawlings got her alone, she would never be seen again. Her only chance was to run, now, while there were still witnesses around.

"Actually," she said, moving toward the back door, "I just remembered I have an important engagement."

"I'm afraid that engagement will have to wait."

Rawlings nodded to his men, who moved to block her escape routes. But Carmen had been planning for this possibility for weeks, and she was ready.

The back door led to an alley that connected to a maze of side streets she'd memorized during her months in Cheyenne. If she could reach her horse, which was saddled and waiting two blocks away, she might have a chance.

"Miss Torres," Rawlings called as she bolted for the door, "I really must insist..."

But Carmen was already running, her skirts hampering her stride but her desperation lending her speed. Behind her, she could hear the crash of overturned furniture as Rawlings's men gave chase.

The alley was empty, but she could hear boots on boardwalks as more men joined the pursuit. They'd been ready for this, positioned throughout the area to cut off escape routes. Carmen's only advantage was intimate knowledge of Cheyenne's back streets and a head start measured in seconds.

She reached her horse as the first shots rang out behind her —warning shots, probably, since they wanted her alive for questioning. But the sound spurred her to greater speed as she untied the reins and swung into the saddle.

"There she is!" someone shouted from a nearby rooftop.

More shots, closer this time. Carmen spurred her horse toward the edge of town, keeping to alleys and side streets, using every trick she'd learned during two years of careful planning.

By the time she reached open country, the pursuit was organized and relentless. But she had the best horse in the territory, and she knew exactly where she was going.

Behind her, Cheyenne burned with the light of torches and lanterns as Rawlings organized a manhunt. Ahead lay the canyon where Cord waited with evidence that might save them all, or might simply provide a convenient place for their enemies to eliminate every witness to Blackwood's crimes.

As she rode through the darkness, Carmen realized that the careful game of investigation and evidence-gathering was over. Tomorrow would bring violence, and the only question was whether justice would survive the bloodshed.

Chapter 16: Violence Escalates

The first shots came at dawn.

Cord was watering his horse at the creek behind Hoffman's ranch when he heard the distant crack of rifle fire from the direction of the O'Brien place, three miles east. The sound carried clearly in the still morning air— not the sporadic shooting of hunters, but the sustained gunfire of men in combat.

He was saddled and riding hard within minutes, his Winchester in his hands and a cold fury building in his chest. For over a year, he'd been Blackwood's unwitting weapon, destroying families through legal manipulation and manufactured charges. Now the mask was off, and they were using actual weapons to finish what corruption had started.

The O'Brien ranch was burning when he arrived.

The house, barn, and outbuildings were already consumed in flames that painted the morning sky the color of blood. Tom O'Brien lay sprawled in his yard, a Winchester beside his body and three bullet holes in his chest. His wife Mary knelt beside him, her dress torn and bloody, trying to shield their youngest daughter from the sight of her father's corpse.

"How many?" Cord asked, dismounting beside her.

Mary O'Brien looked up at him with eyes that had seen too much. "Six men. Maybe seven. They rode in shooting, said we had one hour to pack what we could carry and get out."

"And when O'Brien refused?"

"He said this was his land, bought and paid for legal. Said he wouldn't be driven off by hired gunmen." Her voice broke. "They shot him down like a dog."

Cord studied the tracks around the burning buildings. Seven horses, shod and well-maintained—not the mounts of drifters or desperate men, but the horses of professionals. The attack had been coordinated, efficient, designed to send a message to every small rancher in the territory.

"Which way did they go?"

"Southwest. Toward the Martinez place."

The Martinez family—a young couple with three small children, trying to build a sheep operation on marginal land that nobody else wanted. If the raiders were working systematically through the resistance families...

"Mrs. O'Brien," Cord said, his voice carrying an edge that made her look up sharply. "Take your children to town. Find somewhere safe and stay there."

"What are you going to do?"

Cord checked his rifle, feeling something cold and deadly settling into his chest. For months, he'd been reacting to events, trying to understand what was happening, hoping to find legal solutions to criminal problems. That time was over.

"I'm going to remind some people that I wasn't just good at tracking cattle thieves."

He reached the Martinez ranch as the attack began.

Six riders had surrounded the small adobe house, firing systematically into the walls while Elena Martinez and her children huddled inside. Her husband Carlos was in the barn, using a pitchfork to drive their sheep toward the back pasture while bullets splintered wood around him.

The attackers were so focused on their targets that none of them noticed Cord's approach from the north, using a dry wash and scattered boulders for cover. They'd grown careless, accustomed to terrorizing farmers and homesteaders who couldn't fight back effectively.

They were about to learn the difference between farmers and professional killers.

Cord's first shot took the lead rider from his saddle, the man tumbling backward with a surprised look on his face. The second shot, fired before the others could react, dropped another gunman who was reloading near the well.

"Where the hell—" one of the remaining attackers started to say.

Cord's third shot answered the question, the bullet catching the speaker in the shoulder and spinning him around. Now the surviving riders were trying to locate their attacker while controlling panicking horses and returning fire.

But Cord wasn't where he'd been when he fired. He was moving, using terrain and shadow, picking his shots with the cold precision of a man who'd spent years hunting dangerous prey. These hired guns might intimidate farmers, but they were about to face someone who'd tracked Apache warriors through mountain country and lived to tell about it.

The fourth gunman made the mistake of trying to flank Cord's position, riding hard around a pile of rocks where he thought the shots were coming from. He found Cord waiting with a Colt .45, close enough to see the surprise in the man's eyes before the bullet took him in the chest.

"Jesus Christ!" one of the survivors shouted. "It's that marshal!"

"Maddox ain't no marshal anymore!" another replied, but his voice carried uncertainty.

They were right that Cord wasn't a marshal anymore. What they didn't understand was what he'd become instead.

The fifth man died trying to retreat, Cord's rifle finding him as he spurred his horse toward open country. The bullet took him high in the back, and he pitched forward over his saddle horn before sliding to the ground.

That left two survivors, both wounded, both trapped between Cord's position and the Martinez family they'd been terrorizing. One of them was the shoulder-shot leader, trying to control his bleeding while keeping his gun trained on the house. The other was a young man, barely out of his teens, who looked like he was reconsidering his career choices.

"You boys have a choice," Cord called out, his voice carrying clearly across the ranch yard. "Ride out now, or join your friends in the dirt."

"Go to hell, Maddox!" the leader shouted back. "Mr. Blackwood pays better than conscience!"

"Maybe. But he doesn't pay enough to die for."

Cord's next shot took the leader's hat off, the bullet passing close enough to part his hair. The message was clear: the next shot wouldn't miss by accident.

The young gunman threw down his rifle. "I'm done! Don't shoot!"

"Smart boy. Now convince your friend to be equally intelligent."

But the leader was beyond reason, driven by pride or fear or the desperate knowledge that failure meant death at Blackwood's hands anyway. He spurred his horse toward the house, probably intending to use the Martinez family as hostages.

Cord's bullet stopped him ten feet from the front door.

The silence that followed was broken only by the sound of wind through the cottonwoods and the distant bleating of sheep. Five men lay dead in the Martinez ranch yard, and two others were riding hard toward the horizon, carrying news that Cord Maddox was no longer the reasonable lawman they remembered.

Carlos Martinez emerged from the barn, pitchfork still in his hands, staring at the carnage with wide eyes. His wife appeared in the doorway, their children clustered behind her skirts.

"Señor Maddox," Carlos said quietly. "Gracias. They would have killed us all."

"Maybe. But this isn't over." Cord reloaded his rifle with methodical precision. "They'll be back with more men, and next time they'll be ready for a fight."

"Then what do we do?"

Cord looked at the dead gunmen, thinking about Tom O'Brien's body in his own yard, about the systematic campaign to drive small operators off their land through violence and intimidation. The legal fiction was over. This was war now, and wars were won by the side willing to be most ruthless.

"You take your family somewhere safe," he said. "Let me worry about the next time."

By noon, word of the Martinez fight had spread throughout the territory. Carmen, riding hard from her narrow escape in Cheyenne, found Cord at Gustav Hoffman's ranch, where the old German was fortifying his buildings and preparing for siege.

"Five men dead," she reported, dismounting beside the barn where Cord was checking his weapons. "That's what they're saying in town. Five of Blackwood's hired guns, shot down like they were nothing."

"They came to murder families," Cord said, not looking up from cleaning his rifle. "They got what they deserved."

Carmen studied his face, noting the hard lines around his eyes, the cold set of his mouth. The man she'd come to love was still there, but something fundamental had changed. The careful, methodical marshal who'd tried to work within the system had been replaced by something more dangerous.

"This means open war," she said.

"It was always open war. We just didn't want to admit it." Cord set down his rifle and looked at her. "How many more families have they hit?"

"Three that I know of. The Yamamoto place is gone—burned out, family missing. The Jensons barricaded themselves in their root cellar and held them off, but their house is destroyed. And the Kowalskis..." She shook her head. "They found the bodies this morning."

Hoffman looked up from where he was boarding up windows. "Mein Gott. How many dead?"

"Too many," Cord said. "And there'll be more unless we stop this."

"How?" Carmen asked. "You killed five men today, but Blackwood can hire fifty more. Maybe a hundred."

"Maybe. But hired guns work for money, not loyalty. And money doesn't help much when you're dead." Cord's voice carried a certainty that made both Carmen and Hoffman stare at him. "They want to play by frontier rules instead of legal rules? Fine. Let's see how they like it when someone shoots back."

As if summoned by his words, dust appeared on the horizon—riders approaching fast from the direction of Cheyenne. Too many riders, moving with the purposeful coordination of men who'd been given specific orders.

"Twenty men," Hoffman estimated, shading his eyes against the afternoon sun. "Maybe more."

Carmen reached for the field glasses Cord had brought from his saddlebags. "I can see Hayes leading them. And that's Deputy Marshal Rawlings beside him."

"Good," Cord said, and there was something in his tone that made Carmen's blood run cold. "I was hoping they'd come personally."

"Cord, there's too many of them. Even you can't—"

"I'm not the same man who spent fourteen months arresting innocent people for Silas Blackwood," he interrupted. "That man believed in working within the system, following legal procedures, giving everyone the benefit of the doubt."

He picked up his rifle, checking the action one final time. "This man knows that sometimes justice comes from the barrel of a gun."

The riders were closer now, close enough to see individual faces, close enough to count weapons and estimate intentions. They came like an army, prepared for siege warfare against a single ranch house.

They weren't prepared for what Cord Maddox had become.

"Stay in the house," he told Carmen and Hoffman. "No matter what happens, stay down and stay inside."

"What are you going to do?"

Cord stepped into the yard, his rifle in his hands and forty years of frontier survival etched into every line of his body. Behind him, the ranch house represented everything decent people tried to build in a harsh land. In front of him, twenty hired killers represented everything that tried to tear it down.

The careful game of law and evidence was over. This was about right and wrong now, and Cord Maddox had finally chosen his side.

"I'm going to remind them," he said quietly, "that some people don't intimidate worth a damn."

Chapter 17: The Evidence

The standoff at Hoffman's ranch had lasted three hours before Hayes finally pulled his men back, carrying four wounded and leaving two dead in the German's front yard. Cord had made his point with methodical precision—approaching the ranch meant dying, and Hayes didn't have enough expendable men to test that proposition further.

But victory in one battle didn't win wars, and Cord knew the respite was temporary. Blackwood would send more men, better armed and more carefully organized. The next attack would come at night, with fire arrows and overwhelming numbers.

Which was why, two days later, they'd moved their headquarters to the old Hendricks place—a abandoned ranch with good sight lines and multiple escape routes, deep enough in the mountains that casual searchers wouldn't find it, but with access to the telegraph lines and shipping routes they needed to monitor.

"The Mexican documents arrived this morning," Carmen reported, spreading papers across the rough wooden table they'd set up in the main room. "My contact in Santa Fe managed to get copies of the original land grants before Blackwood's lawyers could destroy them."

Cord examined the documents, noting the official seals and elaborate calligraphy that marked genuine Mexican government papers. Carmen's family had indeed owned fifty thousand acres under a legitimate grant dating to

1821, with boundaries clearly marked and witnesses properly recorded.

"This proves the territorial court ruling was fraudulent," he said.

"More than that." Carmen pointed to specific passages in the Spanish text. "The grant included mineral rights and water access—everything Blackwood needed for his railroad contracts. Without our land, his shipping operation couldn't function efficiently."

Gustav Hoffman looked up from the shipping manifests he'd been analyzing. "These railroad records, they show the same pattern. Cattle shipments increasing precisely when small ranches are eliminated."

Over the past week, their evidence had grown from a collection of suspicious documents to a comprehensive proof of systematic fraud. Working together, the survivors of Blackwood's campaign had compiled a dossier that would destroy the entire network—if they could get it to honest authorities.

"The brand registrations are the smoking gun," said Elena Martinez, who'd joined them after her family's ranch was attacked. "Look at this pattern."

She'd created a timeline showing how new brand registrations coincided with arrests of small ranchers. Within days of each marshal's raid, similar brands would be registered to shell companies, always through the same Denver law firm that represented Blackwood's interests.

"Eighteen families destroyed," she continued, "and eighteen new brands registered to 'legitimate' operations that just happened to have exactly the right cattle to fill Blackwood's shipping contracts."

Thomas Running Bear, who'd been studying the Indian Agency correspondence, added his own evidence to the pile. "The reservation thefts follow the same timeline. Our cattle disappear, your marshals arrest convenient scapegoats, and the animals end up in Blackwood's shipping manifests within a week."

"How many head total?" Cord asked.

"Over four thousand cattle, six hundred horses, unknown numbers of sheep and other livestock." Running Bear's voice was grim. "Market value approaching one hundred thousand dollars."

One hundred thousand dollars stolen through systematic fraud, using federal and territorial authority to legitimize theft on a massive scale. The scope was staggering, but the evidence was equally comprehensive.

"The financial records are just as damning," Carmen added, producing another set of documents. "Bank drafts showing payments to territorial officials, railroad executives, even some federal marshals. All traced back to accounts controlled by Blackwood's operation."

"How did you get these?" Cord asked.

"My contact at the Denver bank. Blackwood's been careless about covering his financial tracks—probably never expected anyone to be in a position to examine them systematically."

They'd been working for hours, cross-referencing documents, verifying sources, building an ironclad case that even corrupt officials couldn't dismiss. But as the evidence mounted, so did the risks.

"We're missing something," Cord said, studying the shipping manifests. "These cattle numbers are too large for just the operations we know about. Blackwood's stealing from more sources than we've identified."

Carmen nodded. "I've been thinking the same thing. The railroad contracts require steady shipments year-round, but the territorial thefts are seasonal. There has to be another source."

"What about the Colorado operations?" Running Bear suggested. "My nephew mentioned cattle drives coming north from the Arkansas River country."

"That would make sense," Elena agreed. "Use the same methods in multiple territories, coordinate through railroad connections, ship everything east through Wyoming."

The implications were staggering. They weren't just dealing with territorial corruption, but with an interstate conspiracy that used federal transportation networks to move stolen livestock across territorial boundaries.

"We need to verify this," Cord said. "If Blackwood's running similar operations in Colorado, we need evidence."

"I might be able to help with that," Carmen said. "My contact in Denver mentioned some irregularities in Colorado shipping records. Mexican families losing their grants through the same legal manipulations we saw here."

"How long would it take to get that information?'

"A few days, if I can get to Denver safely."

"Too dangerous," Cord objected. "Blackwood's people are watching every railroad station between here and Colorado."

"Then we use the evidence we have," Hoffman suggested. "This is already enough to bring down the territorial operation."

But Cord was thinking about larger implications. If they only exposed the Wyoming conspiracy, Blackwood could simply move his base of operations to Colorado or Nebraska, start the whole process over with new officials and different methods.

"We need everything," he decided. "The complete network, all the territories involved, every corrupt official from local sheriffs to federal marshals."

"That could take weeks," Elena protested. "We don't have weeks. After the attack on my ranch, after what happened at Hoffman's place, they know we're organized. They'll hit us with everything they have before we can gather more evidence."

She was right. The window for investigation was closing rapidly. Soon they'd be fighting for their lives instead of building legal cases.

"What about Marshal Garrett?" Running Bear asked. "You said he might be honest federal authority."

Cord had been wondering the same thing. Garrett had never appeared at the canyon meeting, which could mean he'd been compromised, or simply that he'd decided discretion was the better part of valor.

"I think Garrett's been neutralized," Carmen said. "I intercepted a telegraph message yesterday from Rawlings to someone in Denver. Something about 'federal concerns addressed' and 'no further investigation required.'"

"Transferred? Reassigned?"

"Probably. Or given information that made him conclude the complaints were unfounded."

The systematic destruction of their investigation was almost as impressive as the original conspiracy. Every avenue for legitimate redress had been blocked, every honest official either corrupted or eliminated.

"So what do we do?" Elena asked.

Cord studied the evidence spread across the table— documents that proved systematic fraud, witness statements that corroborated theft, financial records that showed corruption reaching the highest levels of territorial and federal authority. Everything needed to destroy Blackwood's operation, if they could find someone with the power and integrity to act on it.

"We need to get this evidence to Washington," he said finally. "Someone high enough in the federal government that local corruption can't touch them."

"How?" Hoffman asked. "Every communication channel we know about has been compromised."

"Direct delivery. Someone takes the evidence east, presents it personally to federal authorities who aren't part of the western territorial system."

"That someone being who?" Carmen asked.

Cord was quiet for a long moment, thinking about the risks and the alternatives. Someone had to carry the evidence out of Wyoming, past Blackwood's network of watchers and hired guns, to federal officials who could act without fear of territorial retaliation.

"Me," he said finally. "I know the territory, I can travel fast, and I'm probably the only one with the skills to get through their surveillance."

"Leaving the rest of us to face Blackwood's retaliation alone?"

"Taking you with me would slow me down and increase the chances of failure. But staying here..." Cord looked around at the faces of people who'd lost everything to Blackwood's operation. "Staying here means watching you all die one by one while I try to fight impossible odds."

It was the kind of decision that had no good answers. Sacrifice the few to save the many, or risk everything on a desperate defense that couldn't possibly succeed.

"There's another option," Carmen said quietly.

"What?"

"We force Blackwood to act precipitously. Make him so desperate to stop us that he makes mistakes, exposes himself to federal scrutiny."

"How?"

Carmen smiled, and there was something dangerous in her expression. "The peak shipping season starts next week. Blackwood's biggest cattle shipment of the year, worth more than all his previous operations combined. If something happened to disrupt that shipment..."

"He'd have to break his railroad contracts," Elena realized. "Lose his preferential shipping arrangements, probably his entire eastern market."

"More than that," Running Bear added. "He'd have to explain to his investors why a year's worth of carefully planned operations suddenly collapsed."

The plan began to take shape as they discussed it. Instead of taking evidence to federal authorities, they would force the conspiracy into the open where federal authorities couldn't ignore it.

"It's risky," Cord warned. "If we attack his shipping operation directly, Blackwood will respond with everything he has. No more pretense of legality, no more careful manipulation. Open warfare."

"We're already at war," Carmen replied. "The only question is whether we fight it on his terms or ours."

Cord looked at the evidence they'd gathered—proof of systematic fraud that would destroy Blackwood's operation if it ever reached honest authorities. Then he thought about the families already destroyed, the people who would die if they waited for legal solutions that might never come.

"All right," he said finally. "We hit the shipping operation. Force them into the open where their corruption can't be hidden."

"And if it goes wrong?"

"Then we'll have died trying to do the right thing instead of waiting for someone else to save us."

As they began planning the operation that would either destroy Blackwood's conspiracy or get them all killed, Cord felt the familiar cold certainty settling into his chest. For over a year, he'd been reacting to events, trying to understand and adapt to circumstances beyond his control.

Now he was taking control, forcing the enemy to react to his moves instead of the other way around.

It felt like coming home.

Chapter 18: The Trap Closes

Silas Blackwood stood at the window of his Denver office, watching the morning sun paint the Rocky Mountains gold, and tried to calculate how much money Cord Maddox was going to cost him. The reports from Hayes had been increasingly disturbing—five hired guns dead at the Martinez ranch, four more wounded in the failed assault on Hoffman's place, and now word that the resistance had somehow acquired detailed financial records of his entire operation.

"How bad is it?" he asked without turning around.

Hayes shifted uncomfortably in the leather chair behind him. "Bad. They've got shipping manifests, brand registrations, even some of the territorial officials' payment records."

"How?"

"The Torres woman. She's been intercepting telegraph messages for months, copying documents, building a comprehensive case." Hayes paused. "We underestimated her."

Blackwood finally turned from the window, his pale eyes reflecting the cold calculation that had built a cattle empire from nothing. At sixty-two, he was still imposing—tall, silver-haired, with the kind of presence that made territorial governors defer to his judgment. But now, for the first time in decades, he was facing an enemy he couldn't buy, intimidate, or eliminate through legal manipulation.

"Where are they now?"

"Holed up somewhere in the mountains. Maddox knows the territory too well—we can't pin them down long enough for a decisive strike."

"Then we change tactics." Blackwood moved to his desk, where a territorial map showed the extent of his holdings. "No more surgical operations, no more careful targeting. We eliminate every small rancher in the territory simultaneously."

Hayes looked uncomfortable. "That's... a lot of families, Mr. Blackwood. Might attract federal attention."

"Federal attention is already here. Marshal Garrett was asking inconvenient questions before Rawlings convinced him to return to Denver." Blackwood's voice was flat, matter-of-fact. "We're past the point of subtlety."

He picked up a telegram from his desk—the message that had convinced him the situation was beyond normal containment methods.

"This arrived an hour ago," he said, handing it to Hayes. "From our contact at Union Pacific headquarters."

Hayes read the message, his face growing pale:

FEDERAL INVESTIGATORS REQUESTING SHIPPING RECORDS STOP QUESTIONS ABOUT TERRITORIAL CATTLE OPERATIONS STOP RECOMMEND

*IMMEDIATE SUSPENSION OF WYOMING
CONTRACTS STOP DALTON*

"They're going after the railroad connection," Hayes said.

"Which means they understand the scope of our operation. Which means Cord Maddox is no longer just a rogue marshal—he's an existential threat to everything we've built."

Blackwood moved to a wall safe, extracting a leather portfolio that contained the real financial records of his conspiracy—payments to federal officials, contracts with territorial commissioners, arrangements with Indian agents. Documents that would destroy not just his operation, but the entire network of corruption that made it possible.

"How much is Maddox worth to you personally?" he asked.

"What do you mean?"

"I mean, how much are you willing to spend to see him dead? Not captured, not discredited—dead, along with everyone who's helped him."

Hayes was quiet for a long moment. "Whatever it takes."

"Good. Because I'm authorizing unlimited resources for this operation. Hire every gun west of the Mississippi if necessary. Burn down every ranch, homestead, and hideout between here and Canada. But end this."

"What about the territorial authorities? The federal—"

"Will be presented with a fait accompli." Blackwood's smile was cold as winter wind. "Sometimes the most merciful thing you can do for corrupt officials is eliminate their need to make difficult decisions."

After Hayes left to organize the final offensive, Blackwood returned to his window, thinking about the empire he'd built through careful application of money, influence, and violence. Seventeen years of patient work, hundreds of thousands of dollars in investments, political connections that reached to Washington itself.

All of it threatened by one stubborn ex-marshal who'd refused to stay bought.

But threats could be eliminated, and Silas Blackwood had built his empire by eliminating threats more efficiently than his competitors.

Cord Maddox would learn that some enemies were too powerful to fight and survive.

The trap began closing three days later.

Carmen was riding the back trails toward Laramie, carrying coded messages for their contacts in the railroad workers' union, when Hayes's men finally caught up with her. She'd been careful, varying her routes, using every trick Cord had taught her about avoiding pursuit. But Hayes had anticipated her movements, positioned men along every possible approach to the city.

She almost made it.

The ambush came at Willow Creek, where the trail narrowed between steep banks and thick stands of cottonwood. Carmen heard the horses moving parallel to her course a moment before the first rider broke from cover, but it was already too late.

"Miss Torres," Hayes called pleasantly as six armed men surrounded her. "You've led us quite a chase."

Carmen's hand moved toward the pistol in her saddlebags, but Hayes shook his head.

"I wouldn't. My men have orders to take you alive if possible, but they're not particular about your condition when we deliver you."

She looked at the faces surrounding her—hard men with the dead eyes of professional killers, men who would rape and murder her without a second thought if Hayes gave the word.

"What do you want?" she asked.

"Information. The location of your mountain hideout, the names of your contacts, the extent of evidence you've gathered." Hayes's smile was genuinely warm. "We can do this the easy way or the hard way, but either way, you're going to tell us everything."

"And if I refuse?"

"Then we start with the families you've been trying to protect. The Martinez children, for instance. Or old Gustav Hoffman. We take our time with them while you watch, until you decide cooperation is preferable to their screams."

Carmen felt something cold settle in her chest. She'd known this moment might come, had prepared herself for capture and interrogation. But the threat to innocent families changed the equation entirely.

"Where are you taking me?"

"Denver. Mr. Blackwood is looking forward to meeting the woman who's caused him so much trouble."

As they rode south toward the railroad, Carmen tried to think of escape options, ways to signal Cord, methods of protecting the information that could destroy Blackwood's operation. But Hayes had planned carefully, positioning guards to prevent any possibility of flight.

She was trapped, and with her capture, the entire resistance was compromised.

The news reached Cord eighteen hours later, delivered by a terrified homesteader who'd witnessed Carmen's capture from a distant ridge.

"Six men," he reported. "Headed south toward the railroad. The woman... she didn't fight them."

Cord stared at the map spread across the table, trying to calculate travel times and probable destinations. If Hayes was taking Carmen to Denver, to Blackwood himself, she had perhaps two days before they forced her to reveal everything.

Two days before every family in their network was hunted down and eliminated.

"We have to run," Elena Martinez said. "Scatter, hide, hope some of us survive until federal authorities act."

"Federal authorities aren't going to act," Running Bear replied. "They've been neutralized or bought off. We're on our own."

"Then what do you suggest?" Hoffman demanded. "Attack Denver? Assault Blackwood's headquarters with a handful of farmers and homesteaders?"

The room fell silent as everyone contemplated the impossibility of their situation. They were outgunned, outmanned, and outmaneuvered by an enemy with unlimited resources and political protection.

But Cord was thinking about something else—the detailed knowledge he'd gained of Blackwood's operation over the past month. The shipping schedules, the security arrangements, the patterns of communication that kept the conspiracy functioning.

"No," he said finally. "We don't attack Denver."

"Then what?"

"I go to Denver. Alone."

The room erupted in protests, but Cord held up his hand for silence.

"Carmen's capture changes everything. If Blackwood breaks her, he'll know about our evidence, our contacts, our plans. Every family in this territory will be dead within a week."

"So we run," Elena insisted. "Live to fight another day."

"There won't be another day. Blackwood's moving to eliminate the entire network, probably planning to blame it all on Indian raids or outlaw gangs. By the time anyone investigates, there won't be enough witnesses left to contradict his story."

Cord began packing his weapons, moving with the methodical efficiency of a man who'd made a decision that probably meant death.

"I know Blackwood's operation," he continued. "I know his security arrangements, his personnel, his methods. If anyone can get Carmen out and expose this conspiracy, it's me."

"And if you fail?" Hoffman asked.

"Then you scatter like Elena suggested, and hope federal authorities eventually figure out what happened." Cord shouldered his rifle and saddlebags. "But I'm not going to fail."

"How can you be sure?"

Cord paused at the cabin door, thinking about the families destroyed, the systematic corruption that had perverted justice itself, the woman he loved who was now in the hands of men who would torture her for information.

"Because," he said quietly, "Silas Blackwood just made this personal."

As he rode through the darkness toward Denver, Cord felt the familiar cold certainty settling into his mind. For over a year, he'd been someone else's tool, manipulated by forces he didn't understand. Then he'd been a reluctant investigator, trying to work within a system designed to prevent justice.

Now he was what he'd always been meant to be—a hunter tracking the most dangerous prey of his career.

Behind him, the resistance scattered to whatever safety they could find. Ahead lay Denver, Blackwood's fortress, and the woman whose capture had finally pushed Cord Maddox beyond the boundaries of law into something far more dangerous.

The trap had closed perfectly.

But traps worked both ways, and Silas Blackwood was about to discover what happened when you cornered the deadliest predator in the territory.

Chapter 19: The Rescue

Denver at midnight was a city of shadows and secrets, where gaslight flickered against brick facades and the sound of boots on cobblestone echoed off narrow alleyways. Cord McBride moved through the darkness like a predator returning to familiar hunting grounds, every sense attuned to the rhythms of a place he'd once called home.

Blackwood's headquarters occupied an entire block on Seventeenth Street—a four-story brick fortress that housed the territorial offices, private security forces, and holding cells that officially didn't exist. Cord had been inside twice before, once as Blackwood's employee and once as his prisoner. He knew the layout, the guard rotations, the architectural weaknesses that money and arrogance had failed to address.

More importantly, he knew Blackwood's mind.

The cattle baron was methodical, predictable in his ruthlessness. Carmen would be held in the basement detention area, questioned by experts who specialized in breaking stubborn prisoners. She'd resist as long as possible, but everyone had a limit, and Blackwood's interrogators were skilled at finding it quickly.

Cord estimated eighteen hours before she broke completely. He'd been riding for twenty-four.

He was cutting it close.

The building's main entrances were heavily guarded, but Cord had spent months studying security arrangements for Blackwood's various properties. The freight elevator on the building's north side operated on a predictable schedule, bringing supplies up from the railroad sidings every two hours. At 2 AM, it would carry coal for the building's furnaces—and one additional passenger that nobody would expect.

Cord waited in the shadows of the rail yard, watching the freight handlers load the elevator car with their usual bored efficiency. When the last bag of coal was secured, he slipped from concealment and dropped silently onto the elevator's roof as it began its mechanical ascent toward the building's basement level.

The shaft was dark, cramped, and filled with the mechanical noise that would mask any sounds he might make. As the elevator rose past the basement level where Carmen was likely being held, Cord forced open the service panel and dropped into the freight car itself.

The elevator shuddered to a stop at the main floor. Through the metal gates, Cord could see the building's central corridor—marble floors, gas lamps burning low, and two guards playing cards at a desk positioned to monitor the main entrance.

Neither man looked toward the freight area as Cord slipped from the elevator car and made his way toward the basement stairwell.

He knew the building's geography by heart: Carmen would be held in one of three detention cells beneath

Blackwood's private offices, areas that were soundproofed and officially designated as storage rooms. The guards would be minimal—Blackwood's arrogance had always been his weakness, a certainty that his power was absolute within these walls.

The basement corridor was dimly lit by a single gas fixture, casting long shadows that provided perfect concealment for someone who understood how to use darkness. Cord moved silently along the brick walls, his Colt .45 ready but not yet drawn. Violence would come, but timing was everything.

He heard Carmen before he saw her.

Her voice came from the third cell, steady and defiant despite obvious exhaustion: "I've told you everything I'm going to tell you. Kill me or let me go, but stop wasting both our time."

A male voice responded with casual menace: "Miss Delgado, we haven't even started the serious questioning yet. Mr. Hayes will be here in an hour with tools that make conversations much more productive."

"I'm looking forward to meeting him again."

Cord smiled grimly. Even under interrogation, Carmen Delgado had more steel in her spine than most men he'd known. But her defiance confirmed what he'd suspected—they hadn't broken her yet, which meant the evidence remained secure.

For now.

The detention area was guarded by a single man seated outside the cell block, reading a newspaper and occasionally glancing toward the cells. Professional, but not particularly alert. Blackwood's people had grown complacent during months of unchallenged success.

Cord approached from behind, moving with the silent precision that had kept him alive through a dozen deadly encounters. The guard's first indication of danger was the cold pressure of a gun barrel against the base of his skull.

"Make a sound and I'll paint these walls with your brains," Cord whispered.

The man stiffened but didn't cry out. Smart.

"Keys," Cord commanded.

The guard reached slowly for the key ring at his belt, his hands trembling slightly. Cord relieved him of his weapons—a Colt revolver and a knife—then struck him precisely behind the ear with the butt of his pistol. The man collapsed unconsciously but breathing.

Carmen's cell was the last in the row, a narrow brick chamber with a heavy wooden door secured by an oversized padlock. Through the small barred window, Cord could see her sitting on a rough wooden bench, her dark hair disheveled but her posture erect and defiant.

"Carmen," he called softly.

She looked up sharply, and her face transformed with relief and something deeper. "Cord? How did you—"

"Questions later. We're leaving now."

He tried three keys before finding the right one, the padlock falling away with a metallic click that seemed impossibly loud in the confined space. The cell door swung open, and Carmen moved toward him with the quick efficiency of someone who'd been expecting rescue.

"Are you hurt?" he asked, checking her arms and face for signs of serious injury.

"Nothing that won't heal." She touched his face briefly, as if confirming he was real. "They threatened the families, Cord. The Martinez children, the homesteaders. That's why I didn't fight them."

"I know. And we're going to make sure those threats can't be carried out."

"How? Blackwood has fifty men in this building, political connections that reach Washington, enough money to buy —"

"Blackwood made a mistake," Cord interrupted. "He brought you here instead of killing you outright. That tells me he's desperate, which makes him predictable."

They moved quickly through the basement corridor, Carmen staying close behind him as they approached the stairwell. But as they reached the main floor, Cord heard the sound he'd been dreading—multiple footsteps echoing from the building's front entrance, accompanied by Hayes's familiar voice giving instructions to his men.

"Search every room, every closet, every storage area. If McBride is in this building, I want him found and killed. If he's not here yet, he will be soon."

Cord cursed silently. Somehow, Hayes had anticipated the rescue attempt.

"Back stairs," he whispered to Carmen, guiding her toward a narrow service stairway that led to the building's upper floors.

But as they climbed, they heard more men entering the building from the rear entrance, their voices carrying clearly in the confined space.

"Block all exits," Hayes commanded. "Nobody gets in or out without my approval."

They were trapped.

Cord paused on the second-floor landing, thinking rapidly. The building had four floors, multiple stairways, and dozens of offices that could provide temporary concealment. But Hayes's men would search systematically, and eventually they'd be cornered with nowhere to run.

Unless Cord changed the rules of engagement.

"Carmen," he said quietly, "do you remember the layout of Blackwood's private offices?"

"Third floor, northeast corner. Why?"

"Because I've had enough of being hunted. It's time to do some hunting of my own."

He began moving upward again, but now his purpose was different. Instead of seeking escape, he was positioning himself for attack.

The third floor was darker than the levels below, with offices that had been closed for the night. Cord knew the territory—he'd walked these corridors dozens of times during his months as Blackwood's employee, learning the geography that was now proving invaluable.

Blackwood's private office occupied a corner suite with windows overlooking the street and alley. More importantly, it contained the safe where the cattle baron kept his most sensitive documents—evidence that could destroy not just his conspiracy, but the entire network of territorial corruption that made it possible.

"What are you thinking?" Carmen asked as they approached the office door.

"I'm thinking Silas Blackwood is about to learn what happens when you corner a man with nothing left to lose."

The office door was locked, but Cord's lockpicking skills hadn't deteriorated during his months in the mountains. Within minutes, they were inside Blackwood's inner sanctum—a room dominated by a massive oak desk, territorial maps covering the walls, and a steel safe that contained secrets worth killing for.

"You know the combination?" Carmen asked.

"No. But I know something better." Cord moved to the desk, opening drawers with methodical efficiency. "Blackwood is paranoid about security, which means he keeps backup records of everything important."

He found what he was looking for in the desk's bottom drawer—a leather portfolio containing duplicate financial records, correspondence with federal officials, and detailed maps showing the extent of Blackwood's illegal operations.

"Insurance," Cord explained. "In case something happened to the primary documents."

Carmen examined the papers, her eyes widening as she realized their significance. "This is everything. Shipping records, payoff schedules, orders for the attacks on homesteaders. We can destroy his entire operation with this evidence."

"That's the plan. But first, we have to survive long enough to get it to the right people."

The sound of boots on the stairs told them Hayes's men were methodically searching the upper floors. They had perhaps ten minutes before the office was discovered.

Cord moved to the windows, checking the drop to the alley below. Three stories, with a narrow ledge that might support their weight long enough to reach the fire escape on the adjacent building.

"Can you make that climb?" he asked Carmen.

She looked at the distance involved and nodded grimly. "If the alternative is Hayes's interrogation, I can make it."

But as Cord prepared to open the window, he heard something that changed his calculations entirely—Hayes's voice in the corridor outside, giving orders to men who were approaching this specific office.

"Check Blackwood's suite first. If Maddox is after evidence, that's where he'll go."

They were out of time.

Cord drew his Colt and positioned himself beside the door, motioning for Carmen to take cover behind the desk. The portfolio of documents was tucked inside his shirt, the evidence that could bring down Blackwood's empire protected by his own body.

The door handle turned slowly.

Hayes entered first, his own weapon drawn, scanning the apparently empty office with professional caution. Behind him came two more men, both carrying rifles and moving with the coordination of experienced killers.

"I know you're in here, McBride," Hayes called softly. "There's no other way out of this office, and my men have the corridor covered."

Cord remained motionless in the shadows beside the door, waiting for the right moment.

"Miss Delgado," Hayes continued, "if you surrender now, I guarantee you'll be treated humanely. Continue to resist, and I'll let my men have some fun before we get around to the serious questioning."

That was when Cord moved.

He struck Hayes from behind, the barrel of his Colt connecting with the man's skull in a blow that dropped him instantly. The second man turned toward the sound, his rifle swinging around, but Cord was already in motion.

The fight was brutal, close-quarters, and deadly.

Cord's first shot took the rifleman center mass, spinning him around into the wall where he collapsed in a spreading pool of blood. The third man got off a wild shot that shattered the office window before Cord's second bullet found its mark.

The gunfire would bring more men running, but for the moment, the immediate threat was neutralized.

Hayes was unconscious but alive, blood seeping from the scalp wound where Cord's pistol had connected. Cord quickly relieved him of his weapons and dragged his body behind the desk.

"Now we climb," he told Carmen.

The shattered window provided easy access to the narrow ledge outside. The night air was cold against their faces as they worked their way along the building's exterior, three stories above the cobblestone alley.

Behind them, they could hear men shouting, doors slamming, and the organized chaos of a search operation that had suddenly become a manhunt.

The fire escape on the adjacent building was exactly where Cord remembered it, but the gap between buildings was wider than it had appeared from inside the office. Carmen went first, making the dangerous leap with the agility of desperation.

Cord followed, the portfolio of evidence secured inside his shirt, and for a moment he hung suspended over empty space with only his grip on the fire escape's metal railing keeping him from a fatal fall.

Then Carmen's hands were helping him over the railing, and they were both safe on the fire escape of a building that Hayes's men hadn't yet thought to search.

"Where now?" Carmen asked as they descended toward the alley.

"Back to the mountains. But first, we're going to make sure this evidence gets to someone who can use it."

"Who? Blackwood owns half the territorial officials, and the federal authorities have been neutralized."

Cord smiled grimly as they reached the alley and began making their way toward the horses he'd hidden near the rail yards.

"Not all of them. And besides, I'm thinking it's time our scattered allies learned they're not as alone as they think."

As they rode through the darkened streets of Denver, heading back toward the mountains and whatever allies they could still trust, Cord felt something he hadn't experienced in months—hope.

The evidence in his shirt could destroy Blackwood's conspiracy, but more importantly, Carmen's rescue had proven something vital: the cattle baron's power wasn't absolute. His empire could be challenged, his plans disrupted, his enemies could strike back effectively.

Behind them, Denver burned with activity as Hayes's men organized their pursuit. But ahead lay the mountains, where scattered families were hiding and where unexpected allies might be preparing to stand together against a common enemy.

The trap Blackwood thought he'd set had backfired. By capturing Carmen, he'd forced Cord to become the hunter instead of the hunted. And now, with evidence that could destroy the entire conspiracy secured in Cord's shirt, the real fight for justice was about to begin.

As they disappeared into the darkness beyond the city limits, neither Cord nor Carmen knew that help was already on the way—help from the most unlikely sources imaginable.

Chapter 20: Unlikely Allies

The abandoned line shack in the foothills twenty miles north of Cheyenne had become an unlikely war council. Cord McBride sat at a rough wooden table studying territorial maps by lamplight, his face bearing the hard lines of a man who'd seen too much and decided that mercy was a luxury he could no longer afford. The evidence from Blackwood's safe lay spread before him—documents that could destroy the cattle baron's empire, if they lived long enough to use them.

Carmen moved quietly around the small cabin, her movements still careful from the bruises Hayes's men had left on her ribs. But her eyes held the same cold determination that had settled into Cord's features during their escape from Denver.

"They'll be watching every approach to Cheyenne," she said, refilling his coffee cup. "Hayes isn't going to let us reach Marshal Garrett or anyone else who might listen."

"Hayes won't be a problem much longer," Cord replied, his voice carrying a flatness that would have surprised the man he'd been six months ago. "Neither will the rest of Blackwood's hired killers."

The sound of approaching horses made them both reach for weapons, but the distinctive pattern of hoofbeats—three riders moving with the steady confidence of men who belonged in this country—told Cord what he needed to know before the first horse appeared in the lamplight.

Thomas Running Bear dismounted first, followed by two younger Lakota warriors whose faces bore the paint of men preparing for battle. The Indian leader's presence filled the small cabin as he entered, his dark eyes taking in the scattered documents and the weapons laid out for easy access.

"McBride," he said simply.

"Running Bear." Cord didn't rise from his chair, but his hand moved away from his pistol. "Didn't expect to see you here."

"Didn't expect to be here. But sometimes the enemy of my enemy becomes my ally, even if I don't trust him."

One of the younger warriors spoke rapidly in Lakota, his tone urgent. Running Bear listened, then turned back to Cord.

"My scouts report Blackwood's men burning homesteads north of Fort Collins. Families with children, old people who never hurt anyone. They're not even bothering to claim it's about cattle theft anymore."

Carmen looked up from the documents she'd been organizing. "How many families?"

"Seven so far. The Martinez place, the Johnsons, old Henrik Sorensen and his granddaughter." Running Bear's jaw tightened. "They burned them out at night, shot anyone who tried to run."

Cord felt something cold and final settle in his chest. The Martinez family had helped them gather evidence, had trusted him to protect them. Now they were dead because

189

he hadn't moved fast enough to stop Blackwood's final play.

"Where are Hayes's men now?" he asked.

"Heading south toward the railroad. Word is they're planning to hit every small ranch between here and Cheyenne before the spring cattle drives arrive."

"Spring drives." Cord studied the calendar tacked to the cabin wall. "That's next week. All the major cattle operations will be bringing their herds through Cheyenne for rail shipping."

"Including Blackwood's," Carmen added. "He'll want to eliminate all opposition before then, so he can ship stolen cattle with no one left alive to challenge the brands."

The cabin door opened again, and Gustav Hoffman entered with two other men Cord recognized—neighboring ranchers who'd lost cattle to Blackwood's operation. Behind them came Elena Martinez, Henrik Sorensen's granddaughter, and half a dozen other survivors of the recent attacks.

The small cabin was suddenly crowded with an unlikely collection of allies: Lakota warriors, German and Scandinavian homesteaders, Mexican-American ranchers, and a few Anglo settlers who'd refused to be bought out or intimidated.

"We heard what happened to the Martinez family," Hoffman said quietly. "Elena got away, told us about the night raids."

Elena Martinez was perhaps twenty years old, with dark hair and eyes that held a rage Cord recognized in his own reflection. Her family's murder had transformed her just as Carmen's capture had changed him.

"They killed my parents while they slept," she said, her voice steady despite the tears on her cheeks. "Shot my little brothers when they tried to hide in the root cellar. I only survived because I was in the barn milking the cow."

The silence that followed was heavy with shared grief and growing anger. These were people who'd lost everything to Blackwood's greed, who had nothing left to lose and every reason to fight.

"What do you want from us, McBride?" Running Bear asked.

Cord looked around the cabin at faces representing every group that had been pushed aside by Blackwood's empire —native peoples whose treaty rights had been violated, immigrants whose homesteads had been stolen, Mexican families whose land grants had been fraudulently canceled.

"Justice," he said finally. "Real justice, not the kind that gets bought off or intimidated into silence."

"And how do we get that?"

"By hitting Blackwood where it hurts most. His money, his reputation, his sense of being untouchable." Cord pulled out the documents from Blackwood's safe. "This evidence can destroy his political connections, but only if it reaches the right people."

Hoffman leaned over the table, squinting at the financial records. "Federal people?"

"There's a Marshal Lucas Garrett who's been asking questions. Real federal marshal, not one of Blackwood's bought men. Problem is, Hayes and his killers are between us and anyone who might listen."

"So we go through them," Elena Martinez said flatly.

Running Bear smiled grimly. "The girl has the right idea. Sometimes the only way to make peace is to win the war first."

Outside, the sound of more horses announced another arrival. This time it was a group Cord hadn't expected— ranch hands and cowboys who'd worked for some of the smaller cattle operations, men who'd been put out of work by Blackwood's systematic elimination of competition.

Their leader was a weathered cowboy named Jake Morrison, whose previous employer had been murdered three weeks earlier in what Blackwood's people had called a "range dispute."

"Heard you were gathering folks who had grievances against Silas Blackwood," Morrison said as he entered the already crowded cabin.

"Word travels fast," Cord observed.

"Not fast enough to save the families that got burned out last night. But maybe fast enough to prevent more killing." Morrison's eyes were hard as flint. "Me and my boys, we know Blackwood's operation. Worked for outfits that got absorbed into his empire, one way or another. We know his schedules, his security arrangements, his weak points."

Carmen looked up from the documents she'd been studying. "What kind of weak points?"

"Well, for instance, most of his hired guns are city boys from back east. Good with pistols, but they don't know the country. And Blackwood himself—he's gotten soft, comfortable, used to having other people do his fighting."

"He won't be comfortable much longer," Cord said quietly.

The cabin door opened one final time, and this arrival surprised everyone. Marshal Lucas Garrett stepped inside, accompanied by three federal deputies whose badges gleamed in the lamplight.

The sudden tension was palpable as hands moved toward weapons and the unlikely alliance prepared for what might be a trap. But Garrett raised his hands peacefully, his eyes taking in the mixed crowd of allies.

"Easy," he said. "I'm not here to arrest anyone. I'm here because I finally found people willing to tell me the truth about what's been happening in this territory."

Cord studied the federal marshal carefully. Garrett was about forty, with graying hair and the kind of steady presence that suggested competence rather than corruption.

"What truth is that, Marshal?"

"That Silas Blackwood has been using fraudulent federal authority to steal cattle, murder homesteaders, and

193

eliminate business competition through systematic violence." Garrett's voice carried the weight of official determination. "I've been investigating reports for weeks, but every witness either disappeared or refused to talk."

"They were afraid of ending up like the Martinez family," Elena said bitterly.

"Which is why I'm here now, instead of waiting for more evidence." Garrett moved to the table where Cord had spread Blackwood's documents. "I understand you have proof of federal crimes."

Cord hesitated. Trusting federal authority had gotten him into this mess in the first place. But Carmen caught his eye and nodded slightly—they needed official backing if they wanted justice instead of just revenge.

"More than proof," Cord said, sliding the portfolio across the table. "Complete financial records, correspondence with territorial officials, orders for specific murders. Everything you'd need to bring down the entire conspiracy."

Garrett examined the documents with growing amazement. "This is... extensive. How did you acquire these records?"

"Does it matter?"

"For prosecution purposes, yes. But for immediate action to prevent more murders, no." The marshal looked around the cabin at the assembled allies. "I have authority to deputize civilians in emergency situations. If you're willing to work within the law, I can give you official standing to act against Blackwood's operation."

Running Bear laughed harshly. "Federal law hasn't been much protection for my people, Marshal. Why should we trust it now?"

"Because this time, you won't be fighting alone. And because the alternative is a range war that will get a lot more innocent people killed."

Cord weighed the options. Official authority would provide legitimacy, but it would also impose constraints on how they could act against Blackwood. And constraints meant some of the bastards might escape justice.

"What kind of authority?" he asked.

"Special deputy marshals with broad enforcement powers. Authorized to make arrests, seize evidence, and use necessary force to prevent federal crimes."

"Necessary force," Cord repeated. "Define necessary."

Garrett met his eyes steadily. "Whatever it takes to stop the killing and bring the criminals to trial."

The cabin was silent as everyone considered the implications. Official sanction versus the freedom to dispense their own justice. Legal protection versus the satisfaction of settling scores personally.

Carmen broke the silence. "The spring cattle drives start next week. Blackwood will be moving his entire operation through Cheyenne to ship stolen cattle east. If we're going to stop him, that's when we'll have to do it."

"In front of hundreds of witnesses," Morrison added. "Cowboys, railroad officials, territorial authorities. If we act then, everyone will see exactly what Blackwood's been doing."

Cord looked around the cabin at the faces of people who'd lost everything to Blackwood's greed. They deserved justice, but more than that, they deserved to survive this fight and rebuild their lives afterward.

"All right, Marshal," he said finally. "We'll try it your way. But understand something—I'm not the same man who accepted a fake badge from Benjamin Hayes six months ago. If your legal system fails these people again, I'll finish this my own way."

Garrett nodded grimly. "I understand. And I hope it doesn't come to that."

As the marshal began swearing in deputies and organizing the evidence that would bring down Blackwood's empire, Cord stepped outside into the cold mountain air. The stars were brilliant overhead, and somewhere in the distance, a coyote called to its mate.

Carmen joined him, wrapping her arms around herself against the chill.

"Do you trust him?" she asked.

"I trust that he wants to stop Blackwood. Whether his methods will be enough..." Cord let the sentence trail off

"And if they're not?"

Cord's hand rested on the grip of his Colt, and when he spoke, his voice carried the promise of a man who'd been pushed beyond mercy.

"Then Blackwood and his people will learn what happens when you corner a predator and give him nothing left to lose."

In the distance, thunder rumbled across the mountains—or perhaps it was the sound of cattle being driven toward Cheyenne, toward the final confrontation that would determine whether justice or corruption ruled this territory.

Either way, the spring shipping season was about to become a reckoning that would be remembered for generations.

Chapter 21: The Shipping Season Showdown

The Cheyenne rail yards stretched for nearly a mile along the Union Pacific tracks, a maze of cattle pens, loading chutes, and switching stations that formed the beating heart of Wyoming Territory's cattle industry. By dawn on the third Tuesday of May, the yards teemed with activity as the spring drives converged from across the territory— thousands of head of cattle, hundreds of cowboys, and enough money changing hands to finance small wars.

Cord McBride crouched behind a stack of railroad ties on the yard's eastern edge, watching Silas Blackwood's operation unfold with the methodical precision of a man studying prey. The cattle baron had arrived before sunrise with his entourage of hired guns, territorial officials, and railroad executives, positioning himself to oversee the loading of what appeared to be legitimate cattle shipments.

But Cord knew better. The evidence spread across the abandoned line shack had revealed the true scope of Blackwood's conspiracy—cattle stolen from small ranchers, brands altered with expert skill, shipping manifests falsified to show ownership by Blackwood's various front companies. Today's shipments would include cattle rustled from murdered homesteaders, animals whose rightful owners lay buried in shallow graves across the territory.

"Target's in position," Carmen whispered, settling beside him with a pair of field glasses. "Blackwood's set up in the main office overlooking pen seven. Hayes is with him, along with Deputy Rawlings and three railroad executives."

Cord took the glasses and studied the office windows. Through the morning sunlight, he could see Blackwood gesturing expansively as he spoke with Union Pacific officials, playing the part of a successful businessman conducting legitimate trade. The sight filled Cord with a cold fury that had been building since Carmen's capture— fury at being manipulated, at the murdered families, at a system so corrupt it protected men like Blackwood while honest people died.

"Federal positions?" he asked.

"Marshal Garrett and his deputies are positioned at the north gate, disguised as cattle buyers. Running Bear's warriors are scattered through the yards, dressed as cowboys and railroad workers." Carmen lowered her voice. "Elena and the other homesteaders are in the crowd, ready to identify their stolen cattle when the time comes."

The plan was simple in concept but deadly in execution. Wait until Blackwood's people began loading the stolen cattle, then spring the trap with maximum publicity. Federal marshals would make arrests based on the documentary evidence while witnesses identified their animals. The entire territorial establishment would see their corruption exposed in broad daylight.

But Cord knew Blackwood wouldn't go quietly. The cattle baron had too much to lose, too many people to protect, and too many guns at his disposal. When the trap closed, violence would follow as surely as thunder followed lightning.

And Cord was ready for violence.

"Movement in pen seven," Carmen reported.

Through the glasses, Cord watched as Blackwood's men began separating cattle for loading, their practiced movements revealing the systematic nature of the operation. Cowboys wearing Blackwood's brand worked alongside men Cord recognized as known rustlers, all of them moving stolen cattle toward the loading chutes with the casual efficiency of routine.

"There," Carmen pointed. "The Martinez family's prize bull. And those longhorns with the altered brands—those belonged to the Sorensen place."

Cord felt the familiar weight of his Colt against his hip, the rifle slung across his shoulder, the knife sheathed at his boot. He'd armed himself for war, not arrest work, because he understood something Marshal Garrett apparently didn't: men like Blackwood and Hayes didn't surrender peacefully when cornered.

They fought like the predators they were, and they killed anyone who threatened their territory.

"Signal Garrett," Cord said quietly. "It's time."

Carmen raised a small mirror, flashing sunlight in a prearranged pattern toward the north gate. Within moments, federal marshals began moving through the crowds of cowboys and cattle buyers, their badges visible now as they approached pen seven with weapons drawn.

"Federal marshals!" Garrett's voice carried clearly across the rail yard. "Nobody move! This is an official investigation!"

The reaction was immediate and violent.

Hayes emerged from Blackwood's office with a Winchester rifle, his first shot shattering the morning air and sending cattle into panicked stampedes. From concealed positions around the yards, Blackwood's hired guns opened fire on the advancing marshals, turning the rail yard into a battlefield where gunshots echoed off steel rails and wooden posts.

But Cord was no longer watching the federal marshals or worrying about legal procedures. The first gunshot had released something in him that months of manipulation and violence had been building toward—a cold, killing rage that transformed him from a reluctant lawman into something far more dangerous.

He moved through the chaos of stampeding cattle and diving cowboys with deadly purpose, his rifle speaking with methodical precision. The first of Blackwood's gunmen died before he realized Cord was behind him, a bullet through the spine that dropped him beside a loading chute. The second managed to turn toward the threat before Cord's rifle put him down permanently.

This wasn't the careful, measured violence of his earlier confrontations. This was the lethal efficiency of a predator unleashed, a man who'd been pushed beyond mercy into something that killed without hesitation or regret.

"McBride!" Hayes's voice rose above the gunfire as the former "Captain" spotted Cord moving between the cattle pens. "You son of a bitch, I should have killed you months ago!"

Hayes's rifle bullet splintered wood inches from Cord's head, but Cord was already moving, using his knowledge of the rail yard's geography to position himself for the killing shot he'd been planning since Carmen's rescue. Hayes had threatened innocent families, had tortured the woman Cord loved, had been the face of Blackwood's corruption for too long.

The Winchester's report was lost in the general chaos of gunfire, but Hayes's scream as the bullet shattered his shoulder was clearly audible. The man who'd manipulated Cord into being an unwitting enforcer stumbled backward, his rifle clattering to the ground as he clutched his wounded arm.

"Please," Hayes gasped as Cord approached with the methodical stride of an executioner. "I was just following orders. Blackwood made me—"

"Blackwood didn't make you torture Carmen," Cord said quietly, his voice cutting through the noise of battle. "That was your choice."

Hayes tried to reach for his sidearm with his good hand, but Cord was faster. The Colt's bullet took him center mass, spinning him into the dirt between cattle pens where he lay still, his eyes staring sightlessly at the Wyoming sky.

Around the rail yard, the battle raged with increasing intensity. Running Bear's warriors fought with traditional weapons and captured rifles, their war cries mixing with the bellowing of terrified cattle. Federal marshals sought cover behind railroad cars while Blackwood's remaining gunmen made their desperate stand.

But the tide was turning. Outnumbered and outflanked, facing enemies who fought with the fury of people who'd lost everything, Blackwood's hired guns began falling back toward the main office where their employer waited.

Cord reloaded methodically, his movements automatic as he calculated angles and distances. Deputy Rawlings was barricaded behind an overturned wagon near pen three, his badge glinting in the sunlight as he fired at advancing marshals. The corrupt lawman had sold his authority to men like Blackwood, had perverted justice for money, had been complicit in murders across the territory.

Cord's rifle found him through a gap in his improvised fortification, the bullet striking with surgical precision. Rawlings collapsed without a sound, another corrupt official eliminated from an equation that had claimed too many innocent lives.

The remaining railroad executives were attempting to flee toward the passenger terminal, abandoning Blackwood as their association became publicly exposed. Cord let them run—they were cowards and functionaries, not the architects of murder. Their flight would serve as evidence of guilt when federal investigators examined the day's events.

But Blackwood himself remained in the office overlooking pen seven, surrounded by his last loyal gunmen and apparently determined to fight to the end rather than face trial.

"Blackwood!" Marshal Garrett's voice carried across the diminishing gunfire. "You're surrounded! Surrender now and you'll get a fair trial!"

The cattle baron's response was a rifle shot that shattered the window of the railway office where Garrett had taken cover.

Cord smiled grimly. Blackwood's refusal to surrender solved several problems at once. A dead cattle baron couldn't buy his way out of prison or have his political allies arrange a convenient escape. Justice delivered by rifle bullet was certain in ways that courtroom justice often wasn't.

He began working his way toward the main office, using cattle pens and railroad equipment for cover as Blackwood's remaining men concentrated their fire on the federal marshals. The battle was nearly over—most of the hired guns lay dead or wounded, the stolen cattle had scattered throughout the yards, and territorial officials who'd been complicit in the conspiracy were either fleeing or surrendering.

But the man responsible for it all still lived, still threatened innocent people, still represented the kind of corruption that turned law enforcement into a tool of oppression.

Cord intended to correct that oversight permanently.

The office building's rear entrance was unguarded, Blackwood's men having positioned themselves to defend against the frontal assault by federal marshals. Cord slipped inside like a shadow, his knowledge of the building's layout from his months as Blackwood's employee now serving a different purpose.

The stairs to the second floor creaked under his boots, but the sound was lost in the gunfire from the front windows. Cord moved down the familiar corridor past offices where he'd once received assignments to harass homesteaders, past the conference room where Blackwood had laid out his plans for territorial domination.

Now those same rooms would witness the cattle baron's final accounting.

Blackwood was at the window of his private office, a rifle in his hands as he fired at marshals in the yard below. Two of his men flanked the window, their attention focused entirely on the battle outside.

They never saw Cord enter the room.

His first shot took the gunman on the left through the head, the man's body crashing into a filing cabinet as he fell. The second gunman had time to turn before Cord's rifle spoke again, the bullet catching him center mass and spinning him away from the window.

Blackwood spun around, his face showing shock and fear as he found himself facing the man he'd manipulated and betrayed. The cattle baron was sixty-two years old, well-dressed, distinguished—and completely out of his element when faced with the lethal consequences of his choices.

"McBride," he said, trying to maintain the authoritative tone that had cowed territorial officials for decades. "You're making a serious mistake. I have friends in Washington, political connections that—"

"Had friends," Cord corrected quietly. "Past tense. They're abandoning you as fast as they can cut their ties."

Blackwood raised his rifle with trembling hands, but Cord was already moving. The Colt's bullet shattered the cattle baron's wrist, sending his weapon clattering across the hardwood floor. Blackwood stumbled backward, clutching his wounded arm, his face pale with shock and pain.

"Please," he gasped. "I can pay you. More money than you've ever seen. Enough to disappear, start over anywhere you want."

"Like you paid me before? To be your unwitting enforcer while you murdered innocent families?"

"That was business! Nothing personal! The territory needs strong leadership, organized development—"

Cord's second shot took Blackwood through the chest, just above the heart. The impact drove the cattle baron backward into his desk, where he slumped forward, blood spreading across the territorial maps that had shown the extent of his illegal empire.

"This is personal," Cord said quietly, watching the life fade from Blackwood's eyes. "You made it personal when you had Carmen tortured. When you murdered families in their sleep. When you corrupted everything law enforcement is supposed to represent."

Silas Blackwood, the man who'd built a cattle empire through murder and corruption, died slumped over maps showing territory he'd never legally owned, surrounded by the evidence of crimes he'd never face trial for.

The gunfire outside was diminishing as the last of Blackwood's men either surrendered or fell to federal bullets. Through the office window, Cord could see Marshal Garrett and his deputies taking prisoners, while Running Bear's warriors helped identify stolen cattle and their rightful owners.

Carmen appeared in the office doorway, her face showing relief when she saw Cord unharmed but concern when she noticed Blackwood's body.

"Is it over?" she asked quietly.

Cord looked around the office where his nightmare had begun months ago, where Blackwood had given him a fake badge and turned him into an unwitting tool of oppression. The cattle baron was dead, his hired guns eliminated or captured, his conspiracy exposed before hundreds of witnesses.

But the railroad executives who'd enabled the scheme were claiming ignorance. The territorial officials who'd taken bribes were burning evidence and distancing themselves from the scandal. The federal politicians who'd protected Blackwood's operation would find ways to avoid prosecution.

Justice, but not complete justice. Victory, but not total victory.

"The shooting's over," Cord said finally. "Whether it's really finished... we'll see."

As federal marshals secured the rail yard and began the complex process of sorting through evidence, stolen cattle, and corrupt officials, Cord holstered his weapons and tried to feel satisfaction in what they'd accomplished.

They'd saved lives, exposed corruption, and eliminated the men directly responsible for murder and theft. But the system that had allowed Blackwood to operate remained largely intact, ready to enable the next ambitious criminal who understood how to manipulate authority for personal gain.

It was justice, partially served. Victory with limitations. An ending that satisfied the need for revenge while leaving questions about lasting change.

Outside, the spring cattle drives continued their flow toward eastern markets, the legitimate ranchers and cowboys conducting honest business while federal investigators tried to separate legal cattle from stolen herds.

The shipping season showdown was over, but its consequences would ripple through Wyoming Territory for years to come.

Chapter 22: Justice Partially Served

The federal courthouse in Cheyenne buzzed with activity in the weeks following what the territorial newspapers had dubbed "The Rail Yard War." Marshal Lucas Garrett occupied a commandeered office on the second floor, sorting through mountains of evidence while telegraph operators transmitted reports to Washington and territorial officials scrambled to distance themselves from the Blackwood conspiracy.

Cord McBride sat across from Garrett's desk, watching the federal marshal organize documents that represented months of systematic corruption. Through the courthouse windows, he could see workmen repairing damage to the rail yard buildings, their hammers providing a steady counterpoint to the legal machinery grinding slowly toward some approximation of justice.

"The good news," Garrett said without looking up from a shipping manifest, "is that we have enough evidence to convict everyone who's still alive and available for prosecution."

"And the bad news?"

"Most of the important people seem to have developed sudden cases of unavailability."

Garrett pulled out a telegram from his stack of correspondence. "Benjamin Hayes disappeared from Denver the night of your rescue operation. Witnesses saw him boarding an eastbound train with several large bags, destination unknown. Deputy Marshal Frank Rawlings left Cheyenne two hours after the shooting stopped, claiming he was pursuing fleeing suspects. He hasn't been seen since."

Cord felt a familiar cold anger at the news, but it was tempered by exhaustion and the growing realization that complete justice had always been an impossible goal. "What about the railroad officials?"

"Ah, that's where it gets interesting." Garrett's smile was bitter. "Marcus Dalton and his associates from Union Pacific have provided sworn statements claiming they were completely unaware of any illegal activity. According to their testimony, they simply processed legitimate shipping contracts and had no reason to suspect cattle theft or brand alteration."

"Despite the falsified manifests? The altered documentation?"

"They claim those were provided by Blackwood's organization, and they had no way to verify authenticity without conducting their own investigations—which, they argue, was not their responsibility as a shipping company."

Cord stood and moved to the window, looking down at the street where life in Cheyenne continued with the same rhythms it had followed before Blackwood's empire collapsed. The territorial capital had a remarkable capacity for absorbing scandal and moving forward as if nothing had changed.

"So they walk away clean?"

"Officially, yes. The Justice Department has decided that prosecuting Union Pacific officials would complicate ongoing railroad development projects that Washington considers vital to territorial progress." Garrett's voice carried disgust. "Unofficially, they've been transferred to other positions and will be watched carefully for future misconduct."

"What about the territorial officials? The commissioners and judges who took Blackwood's money?"

"That's... complicated." Garrett pulled out another file. "Judge Harrison claims the payments were legitimate campaign contributions. Commissioner Walsh says he was consulting on territorial development projects. Senator Bradley's office issued a statement expressing shock at the allegations and noting his consistent support for law enforcement."

The pattern was depressingly familiar. Men with political connections and legal expertise finding ways to reframe criminal activity as legitimate business, using their positions to avoid the consequences that ordinary citizens would face.

"How many actual prosecutions?"

"Seventeen of Blackwood's hired guns who survived the battle, assuming they can be convicted of specific crimes rather than just association with criminal activity. Three territorial clerks who were directly involved in document forgery. And..." Garrett hesitated.

"And?"

"Silas Blackwood himself, posthumously. His estate will face civil forfeiture proceedings, though his lawyers are already arguing that his business activities were legitimate and that any criminal behavior was conducted by rogue employees without his knowledge."

Cord turned from the window, his face showing the kind of cold amusement that had nothing to do with humor. "Blackwood's going to be exonerated by his own death?"

"It's possible. Dead men can't testify to their criminal intent, and expensive lawyers are very good at creating reasonable doubt about the motivations of deceased clients."

The courthouse door opened, and Carmen entered carrying a leather satchel full of documents. She'd spent the past two weeks helping federal investigators sort through the evidence from Blackwood's operation, her knowledge of telegraph systems and territorial records proving invaluable in tracing the conspiracy's scope.

"How did the meeting with the homesteaders go?" Garrett asked.

Carmen's expression was carefully neutral. "Mixed results. The federal government will return stolen cattle that can be definitively identified through brand evidence. Families who lost their land through fraudulent legal proceedings can file for restoration, but they'll have to prove their case in territorial courts using whatever documentation survived."

"Which means most of them will get nothing," Cord said flatly.

"Elena Martinez will get her family's surviving cattle and the deed to land that wasn't burned when her parents were murdered. Gustav Hoffman will have his ownership of his homestead confirmed officially. The Sorensen place..." Carmen shrugged. "Henrik's granddaughter will inherit land with a clear title, but she's a twenty-year-old woman with no family and no resources to work a ranch."

"What about the families who died? The people who were murdered for their land?"

"Their deaths will be officially acknowledged as criminal acts committed by Silas Blackwood's organization. The territorial government will provide modest compensation to surviving relatives, assuming any can be located."

Garrett looked up from his paperwork. "It's not complete justice, but it's more than these families had before. The system worked, partially."

"The system failed," Cord replied quietly. "We got some justice despite the system, not because of it."

The federal marshal studied Cord's face, noting the changes that months of violence and betrayal had carved into his features. "You did good work, McBride. The deputy marshal commission is permanent if you want it. Federal law enforcement could use someone with your skills and experience."

"My experience manipulating honest people into becoming unwitting tools of corruption?"

"Your experience fighting corruption when you recognized it. Your willingness to risk everything for justice."

Carmen moved to stand beside Cord at the window, her presence a reminder of everything the fight against Blackwood had cost and gained. "What will you do now?" she asked quietly.

It was a question Cord had been avoiding for weeks. The battle at the rail yard had satisfied his need for violent justice against the men who'd manipulated and betrayed him. But the aftermath had revealed the limitations of any individual's ability to change a system designed to protect the powerful and exploit the vulnerable.

"I don't know," he admitted. "Part of me wants to take Garrett's offer, try to work within federal law enforcement to prevent future Blackwoods from gaining power."

"And the other part?"

"The other part thinks I've seen enough of what badges and authority really mean. Maybe it's time to find some other way to make a living that doesn't involve choosing between corruption and violence."

Through the window, they could see Thomas Running Bear and several other Lakota warriors mounting horses outside the courthouse. The federal government had confirmed that their treaty rights had been violated by Blackwood's cattle operations, and promised that future incursions would be prevented by increased federal oversight.

But everyone understood that promises were only as good as the political will to enforce them, and political will shifted with changing administrations and evolving territorial priorities.

"What about Running Bear's people?" Cord asked.

"They'll return to their reservation with official assurances that their territorial boundaries will be respected," Garrett replied. "Whether those assurances prove meaningful in practice... that depends on factors beyond my control."

Carmen began organizing documents in her satchel, her movements suggesting preparation for departure. "I'll be leaving Cheyenne tomorrow," she said without looking at either man.

The announcement hit Cord like a physical blow, though he'd been expecting it for days. With Blackwood dead and the immediate conspiracy exposed, Carmen's mission in Wyoming Territory was complete. Her family's land grants could never be restored, but at least the man responsible for their loss had paid the ultimate price.

"Back to Mexico?" he asked.

"Santa Fe first, to report to the families who sent me here. Then probably El Paso, where my cousin has a telegraph office and might have work for someone with my skills."

"You could stay," Cord said quietly. "Help rebuild what Blackwood destroyed. Work with the homesteaders who got their land back."

Carmen met his eyes, and he saw the same awareness there that he felt—love complicated by circumstances that couldn't be changed through willpower or good intentions.

"I could stay," she agreed. "And you could come with me to New Mexico. Start over in a place where neither of us has history with corrupt marshals and cattle barons."

"We could."

But neither of them moved to close the distance between possibility and decision. They loved each other—that truth had been forged through shared danger and mutual trust—but love alone couldn't bridge the gap between their different worlds and divergent purposes.

Carmen was returning to fight for her people's rights in territories where Mexican families still faced systematic dispossession. Cord was contemplating whether law enforcement could ever be reformed enough to serve justice rather than power.

They belonged in different battles, even if their hearts belonged to each other.

"Marshal Garrett," Carmen said formally, "I've prepared a complete report on telegraph intercepts and communications that might be useful in future investigations. The patterns of corruption we uncovered here exist in other territories where railroad development coincides with territorial government weakness."

"Thank you. The Justice Department will find that information valuable."

Carmen handed over her satchel and moved toward the door, pausing to look back at Cord. "Walk me to the hotel?"

They left the courthouse together, stepping into the late afternoon sunlight of a Cheyenne street that looked exactly as it had six months earlier, when Cord had first accepted Benjamin Hayes's offer of a badge and steady pay. The same buildings, the same mixture of cowboys and businessmen, the same sense of a territory balanced between lawlessness and civilization.

But everything had changed, including the man walking beside Carmen toward her final night in Wyoming Territory.

"Do you regret any of it?" she asked as they reached the hotel steps.

Cord considered the question carefully. The violence, the betrayal, the discovery that law enforcement could be purchased as easily as any other commodity—all of it had left scars that would never fully heal.

But the alternative had been to remain Blackwood's unwitting tool, to continue facilitating the dispossession and murder of innocent families while believing he served justice.

"I regret that we didn't figure it out sooner," he said finally. "I regret that good people died while I was still playing by rules that were rigged from the beginning."

"And us?"

"I could never regret us. Even knowing how it ends."

Carmen touched his face gently, her fingers tracing the lines that violence and responsibility had carved around his eyes.

"It doesn't have to end badly," she said. "We could have tonight. And we could remember each other as people who fought for something worthwhile, even if we couldn't save everything."

That night, they made love with the desperate intensity of people who understood that some connections transcend circumstances while being ultimately defeated by them. They talked until dawn about possible futures, alternative choices, and the dreams that brought them together and pulled them apart.

And when the morning train carried Carmen south toward Santa Fe and the life that waited for her there, Cord stood on the platform watching until the last car disappeared beyond the horizon.

Justice had been partially served. The immediate corruption had been exposed. Some families had recovered their rights and property.

But the system that had enabled Blackwood remained largely intact, ready to accommodate the next ambitious criminal who understood how to manipulate authority for personal gain.

As Cord walked back toward the courthouse where Marshal Garrett waited with unanswered questions about his future, he carried the weight of partial victory and the knowledge that complete justice might always remain beyond reach.

The badge in his pocket felt heavier than it had six months earlier, when he'd believed that authority and righteousness were the same thing.

Now he knew better.

Whether that knowledge would drive him toward continued service or permanent retirement from law enforcement remained an open question—one that would have to be answered in the days and weeks ahead, as Wyoming Territory continued its complicated progress toward statehood and civilization.

Chapter 23: The Bitter Victory

Three weeks after Carmen's departure, Cord McBride stood in the cemetery outside Cheyenne, reading the names carved into weathered wooden crosses that marked the graves of families destroyed by Silas Blackwood's ambition. The Martinez family lay beneath a single large stone that Elena had commissioned with money from the sale of recovered cattle. Gustav Hoffman rested beside his wife, finally reunited after months of fighting alone to protect their homestead.

The morning was crisp with the promise of autumn, and Cord could hear the distant sound of hammers as Cheyenne continued its relentless expansion. New buildings, new businesses, new opportunities for the kind of men who understood that territorial governments were more suggestion than law.

"They got some justice," he said aloud, though no one was there to hear. "Not enough, but some."

The federal government's final report had been delivered the previous week, a document that managed to acknowledge systematic corruption while somehow concluding that most of the responsible parties had acted within the bounds of territorial law. Seventeen convictions, modest financial settlements for surviving families, and assurances that such abuses would be prevented in the future through enhanced federal oversight.

It was more than these families had possessed six months ago, when they'd faced Blackwood's predation alone and unprotected. But it fell far short of the comprehensive justice that their sacrifices deserved.

Elena Martinez had used her settlement money to purchase a small ranch north of Fort Collins, determined to rebuild what her family had lost. She'd offered Cord a job as foreman, steady work helping her establish an honest cattle operation in territory that had seen too much dishonesty.

He'd declined politely, unable to explain that the sight of cattle brands and shipping manifests still triggered memories of manipulation and betrayal.

Gustav Hoffman's homestead had been deeded to his surviving grandson, a young man from Kansas who'd arrived on the morning train with plans to honor his grandfather's legacy. He'd also offered Cord employment, managing a ranch that would serve as a monument to the kind of stubborn integrity that had cost Gustav his life.

That offer, too, had been declined.

The problem wasn't the work itself, or the people offering it. The problem was something deeper, a fundamental question about whether honest operations could survive in a system designed to reward the ruthless and protect the connected.

Cord left the cemetery and walked back toward town, passing the rail yards where the spring cattle drives had converged for their final accounting. The pens were nearly empty now, most of the legitimate ranchers having completed their shipments and returned to their ranges. But the infrastructure remained—the loading chutes and switching stations and telegraph lines that would facilitate next year's trade.

And next year, there would be new opportunities for men like Blackwood to exploit the gap between territorial law and federal oversight, new chances to manipulate the system for personal gain.

Marshal Lucas Garrett had made his offer permanent and official, backing it with recommendations from Washington that would guarantee Cord advancement within federal law enforcement. The badge carried real authority, decent pay, and the opportunity to investigate corruption wherever it appeared in the western territories.

But it also carried the weight of working within institutions that had enabled Blackwood's crimes for years before finally acting to stop them. Federal marshals answered to political appointees who answered to congressmen who answered to business interests that viewed territorial development as more important than territorial justice.

Cord reached the main street of Cheyenne and paused outside the Federal Building where Garrett maintained his temporary office. Through the windows, he could see the marshal working at his desk, preparing reports that would justify the limited scope of prosecutions and recommend policy changes that might prevent future abuses.

Good work, necessary work, but ultimately constrained by the same political realities that had protected most of Blackwood's confederates from meaningful consequences.

The door opened and Thomas Running Bear emerged, carrying an official envelope that probably contained assurances about treaty enforcement and territorial boundary protection. The Lakota leader noticed Cord and approached with the measured stride of a man who'd learned not to expect much from federal promises.

"McBride," he said simply.

"Running Bear. How did the meeting go?"

"About as expected. Many words about justice and protection, fewer specifics about enforcement and consequences." The Indian leader's smile was bitter. "My people have heard such promises before."

"But this time is different?"

"This time, we have federal attention and documented violations. That provides more protection than we've had in years past." Running Bear studied Cord's face. "Whether it provides enough protection depends on factors beyond our control."

They stood in comfortable silence, two men who'd fought beside each other against a common enemy and understood the limitations of their victory.

"What will you do now?" Running Bear asked.

It was the question everyone seemed to be asking, and Cord still didn't have a satisfactory answer.

"I don't know. Garrett wants me to stay on as a federal marshal. There's good work to be done, corruption to investigate, justice to pursue within the constraints of law."

"But?"

"But I'm not sure I can work within a system that considers Blackwood's death adequate justice for the families he murdered."

Running Bear nodded slowly. "My people have similar concerns about working within treaty frameworks that have been violated whenever convenient. Sometimes the system provides protection, sometimes it provides the illusion of protection while enabling further exploitation."

"How do you decide when to trust it?"

"We don't trust it. We use it when it serves our purposes and prepare for the times when it doesn't." The Lakota leader's expression grew thoughtful. "Perhaps the question isn't whether to trust the system, but how to work both within and outside it simultaneously."

After Running Bear departed, Cord walked to the small hotel where he'd maintained a room during the federal investigation. His possessions fit into a single saddlebag— weapons, spare clothes, and the few personal items he'd accumulated during his months as Blackwood's unwitting enforcer.

On the table beside his bed lay two letters that had arrived with the morning mail.

The first was from Carmen, written from Santa Fe where she'd found work with a law firm representing Mexican families fighting land grant fraud. Her letter was warm but careful, describing her new work without dwelling on personal feelings or future possibilities.

The patterns we uncovered in Wyoming exist throughout the territories, she'd written. *Systematic dispossession disguised as legal proceedings, territorial governments that serve corporate interests rather than territorial residents. There is much work to be done, and not enough people willing to do it.*

The second letter was from an unexpected source—a law firm in Denver representing Blackwood's estate. The cattle baron's lawyers were offering to settle potential civil claims arising from Cord's "wrongful termination" and "defamation of character" during the federal investigation.

Five thousand dollars to sign a document stating that his employment with Blackwood's organization had been satisfactory and that any subsequent allegations of criminal activity were based on misunderstandings rather than deliberate wrongdoing.

Cord read the offer twice, then struck a match and watched the paper burn in the hotel room's washbasin. Even in death, Blackwood was trying to buy silence about his crimes, using money to rewrite history and protect his legacy from the truth.

Some things couldn't be purchased, corrupted, or compromised away.

As afternoon faded toward evening, Cord found himself at the Frontier Saloon where he'd spent his first night in

Cheyenne six months earlier. The same bartender, the same mixture of cowboys and businessmen, the same undercurrent of ambition and opportunity that defined territorial life.

But he was no longer the broke, desperate man who'd accepted Benjamin Hayes's offer of a badge and steady pay. The months of violence and betrayal had changed him in ways that went deeper than scars or experience.

He'd learned that authority could be purchased, that justice was often subordinate to political convenience, that good intentions were insufficient protection against systematic corruption. But he'd also learned that individuals could fight back, that evidence and courage could expose even well-connected conspiracies, that some victories were possible even within imperfect systems.

The question was what to do with that knowledge.

"McBride!" A familiar voice called from across the saloon.

Marshal Garrett approached, carrying two glasses of whiskey and wearing the expression of a man preparing for a difficult conversation.

"Thought I might find you here," Garrett said, settling into the opposite chair. "You've been avoiding my office for three days."

"Been thinking."

"About my offer?"

"About a lot of things." Cord accepted the whiskey but didn't drink immediately. "Tell me something, Marshal. Do you believe what we accomplished was worth the cost?"

Garrett considered the question carefully. "Seventeen men will go to prison who would otherwise have continued committing crimes. Several families recovered property that had been stolen from them. A major criminal conspiracy was exposed and dismantled."

"And the men who enabled that conspiracy? The territorial officials who took bribes, the federal politicians who provided protection, the business leaders who profited from systematic theft and murder?"

"Most of them will escape legal consequences, yes."

"So we eliminated the hired guns and front men while the real architects of corruption remained untouchable."

Garrett's expression grew troubled. "The system has limitations, McBride. We work within those limitations to achieve whatever justice is possible."

"Or we work outside the system to achieve the justice that institutions can't or won't provide."

"That's vigilantism. Once you abandon legal procedures, you become no different from the criminals you're fighting."

Cord thought about Hayes's death in Blackwood's office, about the methodical violence he'd used to eliminate threats to innocent families. There had been no legal procedures, no due process, no opportunity for corrupt lawyers to create reasonable doubt about guilt.

But there had been justice of a sort—immediate, personal, final.

"Sometimes legal procedures protect the guilty more than they serve the innocent," he said quietly.

"And sometimes they're the only thing preventing chaos and vigilante rule." Garrett leaned forward. "I know you're disillusioned, and you have every right to be. But walking away from law enforcement means abandoning the field to men like Blackwood."

"Staying in law enforcement means accepting limitations that allow men like Blackwood to operate until someone gets lucky enough to stop them."

They drank in silence, each man understanding the other's perspective while remaining convinced of his own position.

"What will you do if you don't take the federal appointment?" Garrett asked eventually.

"I don't know," Cord admitted. "Find some other way to make a living that doesn't require choosing between corruption and compromise."

"Such as?"

"Ranch work, maybe. Honest labor for honest pay, without badges or authority or the temptation to abuse power for personal gain."

But even as he said it, Cord knew that simple solutions weren't available to him anymore. He'd seen too much of how territorial society functioned to believe that ranch work would insulate him from the larger questions of justice and corruption.

The problems that had created Blackwood's empire existed throughout the territories, wherever rapid development outpaced legal infrastructure and federal oversight remained distant and sporadic. Other communities faced similar threats from other ambitious criminals who understood how to manipulate authority for personal gain.

Walking away meant abandoning those communities to whatever protection they could provide for themselves.

Staying meant accepting the limitations of a system that considered partial justice adequate resolution for systematic crimes.

Garrett finished his whiskey and stood to leave. "You don't have to decide tonight, McBride. Take whatever time you need to think it through. But remember—perfect justice may be impossible, but imperfect justice is still better than no justice at all."

After the marshal departed, Cord remained at his table, watching the saloon's evening crowd and thinking about the choices that had brought him to this moment. Six months ago, he'd been a broke ex-soldier looking for steady work and a sense of purpose.

Now he was a man who'd killed without hesitation, who'd seen the mechanisms of corruption from the inside, who'd learned that love and justice were both more complicated and more fragile than he'd understood.

The badge in his pocket represented an opportunity to continue fighting corruption within legal constraints, accepting partial victories and systematic limitations as the price of working within established institutions.

But it also represented the same kind of authority that Hayes had used to manipulate him, the same system that had protected Blackwood's crimes for years before finally acting to stop them.

As midnight approached and the saloon began to empty, Cord made his decision.

He would leave Cheyenne, but not to accept simple ranch work or comfortable retirement from the larger questions of justice and corruption. He would leave to find another way to fight—one that didn't require badges or official authority or the compromises that came with institutional employment.

There were other territories, other communities facing threats from men like Blackwood. Places where federal oversight was even more limited, where territorial governments were even more susceptible to corruption, where good people needed protection that legal institutions couldn't or wouldn't provide.

Perhaps individual action, freed from institutional constraints, could achieve the kind of comprehensive justice that official law enforcement seemed unable to deliver.

It was a dangerous path, one that led toward vigilantism and the kind of violence that solved immediate problems while creating larger ones. But it was also a path that offered the possibility of real change, of justice delivered personally rather than filtered through political considerations and legal technicalities.

The next morning, Cord would pack his saddlebag, leave his federal deputy commission on Marshal Garrett's desk, and ride out of Cheyenne toward whatever opportunity or obligation waited in the vast territories beyond Wyoming's borders.

He was still searching for something he couldn't quite name—a way to serve justice without serving institutions, a method of protecting the innocent without enabling the guilty, a purpose that satisfied both his need for meaningful work and his hard-earned skepticism about authority.

Whether such a thing existed remained to be discovered.

But the search itself had become more important than the comfort of accepting imperfect solutions or abandoning the field entirely to men with fewer scruples and different motivations.

As Cord climbed the stairs to his hotel room, he carried the weight of partial victory and the uncertainty of an undefined future.

Tomorrow would bring new choices, new challenges, and new opportunities to discover what kind of man he'd become through months of violence, betrayal, and hard-earned wisdom about the distance between justice and law.

The badge would remain behind, but the search for something better would continue.

Chapter 24: New Hope

The morning train from Denver pulled into Cheyenne with its usual complement of territorial businessmen, federal officials, and eastern investors drawn by Wyoming's promise of opportunity and development. Among the passengers who stepped onto the platform was a young woman whose traveling dress and confident bearing marked her as someone accustomed to comfort but not afraid of challenges.

Victoria Caldwell was twenty-six years old, tall and fair-haired, with the kind of intelligent eyes that suggested she'd received the education most women of her generation were denied. She carried herself with the poise of someone who'd grown up in Boston drawing rooms but possessed the practical strength that came from actually listening when her rancher uncle had written about territorial life.

Cord McBride watched her from the window of the Federal Building, where he'd come to leave his deputy marshal commission on Lucas Garrett's desk. The marshal was in Denver, testifying before a territorial committee about the Blackwood investigation, which meant Cord could resign without enduring another conversation about duty, justice, and working within imperfect systems.

The young woman on the platform was clearly looking for someone, consulting a letter while studying the faces of men who might be meeting her train. When no one approached, she gathered her bags with determined efficiency and began walking toward the main street.

Cord had seen that kind of purposeful movement before—in Carmen, in Elena Martinez, in women who understood that territorial life required self-reliance more than social conventions. Something about Victoria Caldwell's bearing suggested she'd come west with specific plans and the resolve to see them through.

He left Garrett's office with his commission letter placed prominently on the marshal's desk and descended to street level, where the morning crowd provided anonymous cover for observing the newcomer's next moves.

Victoria entered the territorial land office first, spending nearly an hour with officials who produced maps and documents for her inspection. From there, she visited the bank, the telegraph office, and finally the offices of Henderson & Associates, the law firm that handled property transfers for most of Cheyenne's legitimate business community.

By afternoon, word had spread through the territorial capital's business community that the eastern woman was Victoria Caldwell, niece of the late Matthew Caldwell, whose ranch north of Laramie had been one of the few operations to resist Blackwood's expansion through honest competition rather than corrupt manipulation.

Matthew Caldwell had died of a heart attack three weeks after the rail yard battle, his lawyer's letter reaching Boston with news that his niece had inherited 40,000 acres of prime grazing land, a substantial herd of cattle, and the challenge of operating an honest ranch in territory still recovering from systematic corruption.

Cord learned these details from conversations overheard in the Frontier Saloon, where territorial businessmen speculated about the young woman's intentions and capabilities. Most assumed she'd sell the property to established operators and return to Boston with a substantial profit. A few wondered if she might be naive enough to attempt ranching herself, providing opportunities for the kind of exploitation that had enriched men like Blackwood.

None of them seemed to consider that she might succeed through competence and determination.

The next morning, Cord was packing his saddlebags when someone knocked on his hotel room door. He opened it to find Victoria Caldwell standing in the hallway, her traveling dress replaced by practical riding clothes that suggested she'd already begun adapting to territorial requirements.

"Mr. McBride?" she asked. "I'm Victoria Caldwell. I understand you were involved in the investigation that exposed Silas Blackwood's criminal activities."

"Among others, yes."

"May I speak with you? I have a proposition that might be of mutual interest."

Cord gestured her into the room, noting that she moved with the confidence of someone accustomed to dealing with men in professional settings. Her education was evident in her speech, but there was nothing affected or condescending about her manner.

"I've spent the past two days learning about my uncle's ranch and the territorial situation that led to his death," she began without preamble. "The lawyers tell me Blackwood had been pressuring Uncle Matthew to sell, using increasingly aggressive methods before your investigation exposed his operations."

"Your uncle was an honest man in a territory that didn't reward honesty."

"Which is why I'm here." Victoria moved to the window, looking out at Cheyenne's main street with the analytical gaze of someone assessing opportunities and obstacles. "I intend to operate my inheritance as Uncle Matthew intended—an honest ranch that proves legitimate business can succeed despite territorial corruption."

"That's ambitious. Also dangerous, given how many of Blackwood's political allies avoided prosecution."

"Which is why I need someone with your experience and capabilities." She turned back to face him. "I'm offering you a partnership, Mr. McBride. Not employment, but an equal stake in building something better than what existed before."

Cord studied her face, looking for signs of naivety or misplaced idealism. Instead, he saw the kind of thoughtful determination that had driven Carmen's fight for justice and Elena Martinez's decision to rebuild her family's legacy.

"What makes you think I'm interested in ranching?"

"Because you turned down Marshal Garrett's offer of permanent federal employment. Because you've seen how territorial corruption operates from the inside and understand the need for alternatives. Because you're still here in Cheyenne when you could have left weeks ago."

She was perceptive, he had to give her that.

"I'm not a rancher, Miss Caldwell. I'm a former soldier and temporary lawman whose most recent experience involves killing people who threatened innocent families."

"Which suggests you understand the difference between justice and law, between protecting people and serving institutions." Victoria's voice carried conviction without romanticism. "I'm not offering you a peaceful retirement from territorial conflicts, Mr. McBride. I'm offering you a chance to demonstrate that honest operations can survive and prosper when they're managed by people who refuse to compromise their principles."

It was a compelling vision—using Matthew Caldwell's ranch as a model for how territorial development could serve settlers and communities rather than distant investors and corrupt officials. Building something positive instead of just fighting against systematic negatives.

But Cord had learned to be suspicious of compelling visions, especially when they required trusting institutions and individuals whose motivations might change under pressure.

"What happens when the next Blackwood decides your success threatens his interests?" he asked. "When territorial officials demand bribes for permits and shipping contracts? When railroad executives offer exclusive arrangements that benefit you at the expense of smaller operators?"

"We face those challenges honestly, document any attempts at corruption, and build alliances with other honest operators who share our principles."

"And if honesty isn't enough? If the only way to protect your ranch and your employees is to compromise those principles or use the kind of violence that courts won't sanction?"

Victoria was quiet for a long moment, considering the question seriously rather than dismissing it with easy optimism.

"Then we make those decisions when we face them, based on circumstances we can't predict from here," she said finally. "But we start from principles rather than compromises, from idealism informed by realism rather than cynicism disguised as wisdom."

Cord felt the familiar tug of purpose, the possibility of meaningful work that didn't require badges or official authority. Partnership with Victoria Caldwell offered the chance to build something positive while remaining prepared for the conflicts that territorial life inevitably produced.

But it also offered another form of constraint—responsibility to an operation, to employees, to community expectations about legitimate business practices. Success would require making the kind of accommodations and compromises that had enabled Blackwood's crimes, just to a lesser degree and with better justifications.

"I'm honored by your offer, Miss Caldwell," he said carefully. "But I'm not sure I'm the right partner for what you're trying to accomplish."

"Why not?"

"Because I've learned too much about how territorial society functions to believe that honest operations can remain honest without becoming isolated or ineffective."

"And because you're not ready to stop searching for whatever it is you're really looking for."

Her perception was uncomfortable in its accuracy.

"What do you think I'm looking for?"

"A way to serve justice without serving injustice, to protect people without enabling the systems that exploit them, to find meaningful work that doesn't require compromising the principles you've developed through hard experience."

Victoria moved back to the window, watching the street activity below.

"I think you're looking for something that may not exist, Mr. McBride. Perfect justice, uncomplicated morality, work that never requires choosing between competing goods or accepting lesser evils."

"Maybe."

"But while you're searching for that impossible standard, real opportunities to do meaningful good are passing you by. My ranch could be one of those opportunities."

She was right, and Cord knew it. But he also knew that accepting her partnership would mean abandoning the search for something more comprehensive, more personally satisfying, more aligned with the hard-earned wisdom that months of violence and betrayal had produced.

"I hope you succeed, Miss Caldwell. Truly. The territory needs more people like you, willing to take risks for principle rather than just profit."

"But you won't be one of them."

"Not yet. Maybe not ever. But I'm not ready to stop looking for whatever comes next."

Victoria nodded, understanding and disappointment mixing in her expression.

"Where will you go?"

"Don't know yet. Maybe Denver, see what opportunities exist in Colorado Territory. Maybe north toward Rapid City, where territorial government is even weaker and federal oversight more limited. Maybe south toward Texas, where different problems require different solutions."

"Running toward something or away from something?"

Cord considered the question as he shouldered his saddlebags and rifle. "Both, probably. Away from the limitations of working within systems I don't trust, toward whatever use I can make of skills I'd rather not have needed to develop."

Victoria extended her hand with the firmness of someone who understood business partnerships and personal respect.

"If you change your mind, the offer remains open. And if you find whatever it is you're looking for, I hope it proves worthy of your search."

"Thank you. And Miss Caldwell? Don't compromise those principles any more than absolutely necessary. The territory has enough people who started with good intentions and ended up serving interests they never meant to enable."

"I'll remember that."

An hour later, Cord rode out of Cheyenne on the same horse that had carried him into town six months earlier, when he'd been a broke ex-soldier looking for steady work and a sense of purpose. The morning sun painted the surrounding plains gold, and the road south toward Denver stretched empty ahead of him.

Behind him, Cheyenne continued its relentless growth, new buildings rising where Blackwood's conspiracy had briefly threatened to dominate territorial development. Somewhere in town, Victoria Caldwell was probably meeting with lawyers and ranch managers, beginning the complex process of turning inherited property into a working operation based on principles rather than expedience.

Somewhere farther south, Carmen was fighting legal battles for Mexican families whose land grants had been fraudulently canceled by territorial officials. Elena Martinez was building a new ranch on recovered property, determined to honor her family's memory through honest success.

All of them were finding ways to serve justice within imperfect systems, accepting limitations and partial victories as the price of meaningful work.

But Cord wasn't ready for that kind of acceptance yet. The violence that had transformed him from unwitting tool into deadly predator had also revealed possibilities that institutional employment couldn't accommodate—the potential for individual action freed from political constraints, for justice delivered personally rather than filtered through corrupt bureaucracies.

Whether such possibilities could be pursued without becoming the kind of vigilante that law enforcement was designed to prevent remained an open question. Whether the search for perfect justice would lead to meaningful work or dangerous isolation was equally uncertain.

But the search itself had become more important than comfortable solutions or easy answers.

As Cheyenne disappeared behind him and the territorial road opened toward whatever waited in Colorado, Texas, or the Dakota territories beyond, Cord carried the weight of hard-earned wisdom and the uncertainty of an undefined future.

The badge was gone, left behind with institutional authority and its attendant compromises. The woman he'd loved had returned to her own battles in different territory. The immediate corruption had been exposed and partially defeated.

Now came the harder challenge: discovering what kind of man he'd become through months of violence and betrayal, and what use he could make of that knowledge in service of something larger than personal survival or comfortable retirement.

The road stretched ahead, empty and full of possibilities.

Behind him, Wyoming Territory continued its complicated progress toward statehood and civilization.

Ahead lay Colorado, or the Dakotas, or Texas—territories where other communities faced threats from other ambitious criminals who understood how to manipulate authority for personal gain.

Cord McBride rode toward whatever obligation or opportunity waited beyond the horizon, still searching for the elusive balance between justice and law, between protecting the innocent and serving institutions, between meaningful work and moral compromise.

The search had become its own purpose, and the territory ahead was vast enough to accommodate whatever he might discover about himself and the justice he sought to serve.

The End

Glossary of Western Terms

Assay/Assayer – The process of testing ore to determine its mineral content and value; the person who performs this test.

Batwing doors – Swinging saloon doors that typically reached from knee to chest height, allowing air circulation while providing minimal privacy.

Boomtown – A town that experiences rapid growth due to sudden economic prosperity, typically from mining or railroad development.

Claim – A parcel of land staked out by a miner, giving them the legal right to extract minerals from that specific area.

Claim jumper – Someone who illegally seizes another person's mining claim, often through fraud, intimidation, or violence.

Drummer – A traveling salesman who "drummed up" business for wholesale companies.

Greenhorn – An inexperienced person; a newcomer to the West unfamiliar with frontier ways.

Played out – Exhausted or depleted; typically used to describe a mine that has run out of valuable ore.

Road agent – A highwayman; a robber who targeted stagecoaches and travelers on remote roads.

Scabbard – A leather sheath for carrying a rifle or carbine, typically attached to a saddle.

Stake – A mining claim; also refers to the funds needed to get started in prospecting or gambling.

Territory – A region of the United States not yet admitted as a state, governed under federal law. Colorado became a state in 1876, five years before this story takes place.

Trace – The leather straps or chains connecting a horse's harness to a wagon or carriage.

Treaty land – Land designated by federal treaty as belonging to Native American tribes, though such treaties were frequently broken or renegotiated.

Vein – A deposit of minerals, especially metallic ore, found within rock formations.

Author's Note:

Shadows Over Cheyenne is a work of fiction. While the novel draws inspiration from real historical events and conditions in the American West during the 1870s and 1880s, all characters and specific events depicted are fictional. The story explores themes of corruption, justice, and individual moral choice within the context of territorial development and the conflicts that arose between different groups competing for land and resources during this period of American expansion.

The systematic corruption and exploitation depicted in the novel, while fictional in its specific details, reflects documented patterns of abuse that occurred throughout the American frontier as rapid territorial development often outpaced legal institutions and federal oversight. The experiences of small ranchers, homesteaders, Mexican landowners, and Native American tribes represent the real struggles of people who found themselves caught between competing interests and inadequate legal protections.

Cord McBride's journey from manipulated tool to independent seeker of justice reflects the broader American experience of individuals trying to find their place and purpose in a rapidly changing society where traditional authorities and institutions were often unreliable or corrupt.

This novel is dedicated to the memory of all those who fought for justice in the American West, both within and outside the formal structures of law and government, and to the ongoing struggle to balance individual conscience with institutional authority in the pursuit of a more just society.

About the Author

Del Wilber is a decorated Navy veteran with a distinguished 20-year career flying the mighty P-3 Orion aircraft as a Aircrewman. He is an autodidact who went on to earn a BS in General Science from Excelsior University, an M.Ed. In Instructional Design from AIU, and a Ph.D. in Education from Capella University. He has also completed many courses from Walden University and Texas A&M. He taught himself to play guitar and learn how to sail. He is an accomplished sailor who prefers single-handed ocean passages and has owned many sailboats. He lives the quiet life at home with his wife, his dog, and a parrot who talks too much.

Also by Del Wilber

Dead Reckoning

Acknowledgments

This book was written with the help of Colorado itself. The aspens, the peaks, the thin mountain air—every mile I traveled through that beautiful, unforgiving country found its way onto these pages.

I'm grateful to the many historical websites, archives, and local historical societies that provided the dates, details, and context needed to make 1881 Colorado feel authentic. Any errors are mine alone.

Finally, thank you to the Western writers who came before me and showed that this genre could be both entertaining and meaningful. Your work lit the trail I'm trying to follow.

www.ingramcontent.com/pod-product-compliance
Lightning Source LLC
Chambersburg PA
CBHW022010010726
47494CB00003B/980